Alexis foun
unlocked the dead bolt and walked
quickly into her parents' house.

For reasons she couldn't explain, the shadows seemed thicker than they had before, closer somehow, pressing down against her and making it tough to breathe. She wanted to call out, but she knew no one would answer, so she didn't bother. Her fingers found the light switch a second later and she flipped it up. Nothing happened. Her mouth went dry as she tried once more. The darkness remained and seemed to increase.

She took a step into the living room, then stopped.

A man dressed completely in black sat in her father's chair. Alexis stared at him in shock, a sense of dread coming over her with such intensity, she felt her entire body go hot. In the span of a heartbeat she was more scared than she'd ever been in her life. She couldn't talk, couldn't do anything but stare at the stranger.

He looked at her through the gloom and spoke in a low voice. "You're Alexis."

Wishing she could answer another way, she nodded.

"I'm Gabriel O'Rourke. I'm here to explain."

Dear Reader,

Losing what you care about most is everyone's biggest
nightmare. For me and, I suspect, a lot of you as well,
that's family. My husband, my parents, my siblings and
their children...all these people are part of who I am.
Their influence has made me the woman I am, and
because of that, much of what I do is a reflection of them.

In this book, my heroine suffers the loss of her family. At a
young age, even as she wants to become independent and
cast off those family ties, sudden circumstances take away
her mother, her father and even her baby brother.

When the man behind their disappearance reenters
her life, Alexis Mission wants nothing to do with him.
Gabriel O'Rourke is someone she's never trusted and
never will. He took from her everything that was important.
How can she ever forgive him, much less trust him? The
answer, as always, lies in love. Through it, all things are
possible, including pardon and understanding.

Families are curious things. Most of us have a love/hate
relationship with those closest to us. Their foibles drive
us crazy, and they never act the way we really think they
should. But when things don't go right, they're usually the
first people we call for sympathy and support. And they
give it—because they love us.

If it's been a while since you talked to your mother, your
father, that crazy cousin who still lives back home, give
them a call when you finish reading this book. Connect
with them and let them know they're in your thoughts. In
the end, families are what matter.

Sincerely,

Kay David

Books by Kay David

HARLEQUIN SUPERROMANCE

Disappear
Kay David

HARLEQUIN®

TORONTO • NEW YORK • LONDON
AMSTERDAM • PARIS • SYDNEY • HAMBURG
STOCKHOLM • ATHENS • TOKYO • MILAN • MADRID
PRAGUE • WARSAW • BUDAPEST • AUCKLAND

ISBN 0-373-71074-7

DISAPPEAR

This edition published by arrangement with Harlequin Books S.A.

® and TM are trademarks of the publisher. Trademarks indicated with
® are registered in the United States Patent and Trademark Office, the
Canadian Trade Marks Office and in other countries.

Visit us at www.eHarlequin.com

Printed in U.S.A.

This book is dedicated to anyone who has lost someone important. Be it by bad luck or choice, long expected or a surprise, the void left behind is one that can never be filled. Once you love, a part of you always loves— whether those you love are present in your life or far, far away. I hope all of you know that time and love helps heal the wound.

CHAPTER ONE

ALEXIS MISSION HADN'T driven a car in more than a year.

She hadn't gone to McDonald's for a hamburger, she hadn't stopped at a mall to shop, she hadn't put on lipstick or worn a pair of panty hose or done any of the countless things Americans did every day without thought.

Coming home was a shock.

She walked out of the Albuquerque airport and into the chilly New Mexican sunshine. Everywhere she looked, people were rushing. The confusion was even more overwhelming on the sidewalk than it had been inside, the cacophony of horns, engines and movement too much for her to absorb. All at once, she felt as if she'd been living on a different planet instead of a tiny village in Peru.

Despite her anxiousness, Alexis threaded her way through the chaos with determination. She *had* to get accustomed to civilization again. Her family didn't know it yet, but she had returned and not just for a visit. She was back home to stay. Her mother's

Thanksgiving invitation had provided Alexis the excuse she'd been looking for for the past six months.

She crossed the walkway to the rental-car buses
and located the proper van. Five minutes later, it
stopped in front of a low-rise building and everyone
jumped out. Moving with the crowd, Alexis found
herself in front of a neatly uniformed agent who had
her stamped and ready to go with an efficiency she
hadn't seen in quite some time. In the lot behind the
building, she located the small red Mazda he'd as-
signed her.

She threw her duffel bag into the spotless trunk,
then climbed into the front seat and fumbled with the
keys. After a second's study, she started the compact
vehicle, but didn't put it in gear. With the motor purr-
ing quietly and the jets rumbling overhead, she simply
sat in the car and thought, just as she had a thousand
times, about the last time she'd seen her family.

Her baby brother had been too young to do anything but cry, his big eyes filled with confusion. A
late surprise for her parents, Toby had been more like
Alexis's own child than a brother. But she'd kissed
his plump cheek and turned away. The pain of that
moment had carved a hole in her chest, but it was the
anger—the *disappointment*—in her parents' gazes
that had haunted her.

When she was nineteen, however, nothing had
meant more to Alexis than Esteban Garza. He was the
only person she could think about. She'd met the

handsome young social worker through a volunteer program in Peru. He was a teacher, doing incredible work high in the Andes, helping his people. She wanted to be his partner—his soul mate—and toil beside him forever. Everyone had been horrified at the thought of her moving so far from home to live with a virtual stranger, but Alexis had felt she was old enough to make such decisions on her own.

Her mother couldn't say too much about Alexis's plans because for years Selena Mission had filled her daughter's head with romantic stories about Lima, Selena's birthplace. The men were all handsome, the women gorgeous, the beauty of the country unparalleled. Alexis's father, Robert, had had plenty to say, though.

"You're too young. You don't know what you're doing... You're throwing away your life, for God's sake..." He'd followed Alexis out of the house the day she'd left, begging her to change her mind, then threatening her when she didn't. "I swear to God, Alexis, if you get in that car, don't bother to ever come back! No daughter of mine would do something this stupid!"

They'd always been close, so the fight with her father had been shocking to Alexis. Angry and ugly. She'd said things she hadn't meant, and so, she hoped, had he.

One way or the other, she was about to find out, and then it'd be her time to beg...for forgiveness and understanding. Her throat tightened in anticipation. What if he ignored her pleas as she had his? Her mother was the one who'd written to Alexis. *Come home for Thanksgiving, Alexis,* she'd scribbled. *We miss you terribly.*

Knowing it would be easier to explain once she was there, Alexis had never replied. She'd simply packed her things and left. Controlling and critical, Esteban had been impossible to live with and impossible to please, his Latin machismo ingrained so deeply their relationship had been doomed from the very start. Her parents had realized that as soon as they'd met him; it'd taken Alexis a year to understand then another six months to admit it.

A commercial came over the car's radio, the volume suddenly jumping, the holiday jingle loud and garish. She clicked off the noise then put the Mazda into gear and carefully backed up. The wheel felt huge in her hands, the brake pedal unwieldy.

In an hour, she reached Los Lobos.

Her parents and younger brother had moved to New Mexico right after Alexis had left for Peru. She didn't know Los Lobos, but she'd seen thousands of towns like it in the years they'd moved around the country. Small and depressed, hanging on to what it'd been in better days. The community was still alive only because of the government think tank where her father and mother worked, along with some of the other top scientists in the world.

Alexis found the neighborhood and then the house. Driving slowly, she passed the brick home and circled the block with her nerves jangling. When she came back around, she slowed the car five houses down.

Her mother's trademark Thanksgiving decoration was hanging on the front door. A diehard optimist, Selena Mission was a brilliant mass neuron scientist, but domestic tasks had always eluded her. Alexis and her father had always teased Selena unmercifully over the strange straw and pumpkin wreath, but seeing it now brought a quick sting to Alexis's eyes.

She dashed away the tears then eased the car into the driveway and parked. Her heart jumped into her throat and stayed there, a lump that only seemed to grow larger. Finally, her hands shaking, she managed to open the door and get out.

On the porch, she paused. Should she knock? Should she ring the doorbell? Should she just stand there and pray someone would come? None of those options seemed right, and after a few more seconds of hesitation, she knocked once then opened the door and called out. "Mom? Dad?"

No one answered, but they didn't have to.

Alexis had found home and she knew it.

The familiar furniture, the sound of the grandfather clock, even the spices filling the air—everything was known and dear. Alexis felt as if she'd been out to grab a gallon of milk at the corner store. The tightness

in her chest dissolved and she started to cry. She
pushed the door open wider and stepped inside.

"Mom? Dad? Toby? Anybody here?"

The only sound she heard was the ticking clock,
the silence beneath it strangely empty. She walked
through the living room and into the kitchen. The
room was unoccupied but the oven was still on.
Cracking the door open, Alexis bent over and peeked
inside to see a turkey. The bird had been cooking way
too long—the skin looked dry and the wings had already fallen off. With a puzzled frown, she turned off
the heat and looked around. Two pies with lopsided
crusts and dimpled tops sat by a window, which revealed an equally unoccupied backyard.

Stepping over a scattering of colorful blocks, her
confusion grew as she glanced into the dining room
connected to the kitchen. The old scarred table was
set with the old unmatched china. For four, she noted
with a catch, her own special glass sitting at the plate
on the right-hand side. "Just in case," Alexis could
hear her mother say. A centerpiece Alexis had never
seen was in the middle, but it had her mother's stamp.
No one else could arrange flowers that badly.

Alexis called out again as she headed toward the
back of the house. Three bedrooms, two bathrooms,
a den. All empty. She stopped at the door to what
was clearly the guest room, her own childhood furniture in place. The bed had been turned back and
there were fresh towels waiting in two neat piles on

top of the quilted coverlet. Her mother had obviously been hoping Alexis might come, even though the invitation had gone unanswered. Alexis turned away, blinking.

What could have taken them away? With a feeling of dread, she had the sudden thought—had someone had an accident…or worse?

Dropping her purse on the chest in the bedroom, Alexis returned to the front of the house where the garage was located. To her surprise, two cars were parked inside. Feeling foolish but needing the confirmation, she went first to the one she recognized—her father's truck—and then to the other one, a new sedan. The registration papers for both cars were exactly what she'd expected, her parents' names listed in black and white.

Walking back into the living room, Alexis sat down, her unease growing. It was too weird, too strange. Where on earth could they be? She argued with herself, thinking up a million explanations for their absence, but none of them made any sense. A tiny voice in the back of her mind told her she was being paranoid, but she ignored it and called the local hospital, getting the name and number from a scruffy directory underneath the phone beside the couch. There was only one facility in town and it took them less than a minute to check. No one by the name of Mission had been brought in.

She waited an hour more then she went to the

neighbors. On the left, an older couple lived. They'd seen nothing, they both said, but would she like to come in and visit until her folks got back? Alexis declined politely and went to the house on the other side. A younger woman answered the door, two crying babies at her feet. She'd just moved in the week before, she explained, and didn't know her neighbors yet.

No one had seen anything. No one had heard anything. No one knew anything.

Wrapping her arms around herself, Alexis hurried back to the house, the evening air growing bitter. What could have made them take off like this? And how had they left? She entered the empty house, a chill coming over her that had nothing to do with the weather. She hesitated for only a second, then she picked up the phone and dialed 911.

The dispatcher didn't know what to make of her.

"Your parents aren't there? How old are you, sweetie?"

"You don't understand!" Alexis said in exasperation. "I'm an adult! I've been gone—for a long time—and they invited me home for Thanksgiving. They're not here, though, and I've been waiting for hours. Has anyone…well, called anything in?"

"What's the address?"

"It's 2550 Red Oak."

Alexis could hear the tapping of computer keys.

"No calls have been made to that address."

"Are you sure? Nothing at all?" She started to explain the circumstances, but she didn't get far. The dispatcher cut her off with a curt question, another phone line ringing in the background.

"Would you like to file a report, ma'am?"

"Not…not right now," Alexis said finally. "But I may call back and do that."

"We'll be here."

Alexis slowly hung up the receiver. In Pricaro, the closest village to where she'd lived, there had been only one telephone. Meant to be used for emergencies, most of the time the line didn't work at all.

She might as well have been back in the mountains for all the good the call had done her.

Reaching over, she picked up a photograph at the end of the sofa table. The picture had been taken at a picnic just after Toby's birth. Selena was holding the baby, Robert's arm slung casually over Alexis's shoulders. She clutched the snapshot, her fingerprints leaving marks on the frame as she rose from the couch and drifted over to the window. Pulling back the curtain, she stared into the darkness.

Where were they?

ALEXIS PACED the living floor for twenty more minutes, then another possibility came to mind. Her parents sometimes worked strange hours—maybe something had come up at their office. It wouldn't be the first time her mom had left the house with the oven on.

Hurrying into her father's study, Alexis searched his desk for an address for the think tank. She found nothing but she wasn't surprised. Her father didn't bother himself with mundane little details like address books. With a groan of frustration, she slammed his desk drawer closed.

A pack of matches, obviously dislodged from somewhere at the back of the desk, fluttered down to the carpet. Alexis picked it up. *Norman's Service Station. Twenty-four Hours, Seven Days a Week.* She opened it and inside, her father's neat printing noted: "Grumpy but helpful." Seeing his handwriting brought fresh concern...and then determination. It wasn't much, but she knew no one in town. Memorizing the address, Alex dropped the matchbook, ran into the living room and grabbed her coat.

Praying the place wasn't closed, Alexis found the gas station ten minutes later, and breathed a sigh of relief. It was open. She jumped from the car and ran inside. The temperature had dropped even more in the past hour and the wind had picked up. The chill cut into her skin and she started to shiver, trying to convince herself it was the weather and not her nerves.

An old man sat behind a grungy counter, his overalls spotted with grease stains, a filthy black cap covering his head. As Alexis came in, he tore his eyes reluctantly from the television set and a grainy football game, then immediately turned back to the screen. "We're self-serve tonight—"

"Are you Norman?"

"Who's askin'?"

"I need directions." Alexis rubbed her cold hands together and blew on them. "To the Mansfield Operations Center. I'm Alexis Mis—"

"They don't let visitors in there."

"I don't care. I've got to go out there and find—"

"Place is closed." He spoke with one eye on the television, then finally gave her his attention when a commercial flashed on. "It's Thanksgivin', you know. S' holiday."

"Surely there's a skeleton staff. I—"

He interrupted her again and she wondered if he ever let anyone complete a sentence. "Who you lookin' for?"

"My parents. Robert and Selena Mission," she answered. "They're scientists at the—"

"Never heard of 'em." He returned to the television as if she'd already gone. *Helpful?* Her father gave everyone the benefit of the doubt but his description had really pushed the limit this time. Alexis gave up. She'd just have to go somewhere else. As she opened the door to leave, the old man spoke one more time.

"Up the highway. Go left. Ten miles outta town."

HE DROVE by the house slow and easy, the paneled van inconspicuous to any curious eyes. The windows in the small brick home were dark and the place looked empty. Relief eased some of the tension in his body, but not all of it. He had a lot of work ahead of him and not enough time to do it in.

Turning left at the end of the street, Gabriel O'Rourke circled back and parked a block over, in front of a home with a For Sale sign in the yard. Opening the vehicle's double back doors, he pulled out a canvas bag printed with a plumbing logo that matched the sign on the van. He let his eyes search the street while acting as if he was getting out more tools. Everything looked quiet enough. Gabriel went to the front porch of the house. Pretending he had a key that didn't work, he stood for a moment, then shook his head in a frustrated way and headed for the back. It took him thirty seconds to jump the fence on the side and shed the white plumber's suit. Thirty seconds after that, he'd jumped the rear fence as well, landing in the Missions' backyard, now dressed in black. He opened the metal panel on the side of their garage and threw all the switches, shutting off the power. The shadows covered his progress a moment later.

As soon as he stepped inside, the awareness hit him. Something was different. Someone had been in the house and had just left. The air still shimmered, as if disturbed by a recent passing. He cursed silently, but he wasn't surprised. Everything that could go wrong with this operation *had* gone wrong.

Placing the canvas bag on the floor, Gabriel removed his .38 from his waistband. With noiseless steps he checked out the interior, foot by foot. Until he came to the extra bedroom. When he saw the bags, he spoke out loud, his violent curse breaking the silence like a rock shattering a window.

The girl had come back. Dammit to hell, she'd come back!

He stared at the bags but he didn't move. For the love of God, if she'd just been a little earlier…or if she'd only told them she was coming…things would have been *so* different. He uttered another oath and closed his eyes, allowing himself a moment of regret.

Why in the hell hadn't he listened to his gut? From the very beginning, he'd had a bad feeling about this operation. Civilians involved. International technology. Bad guys who went beyond bad. The ill-conceived fiasco had been doomed from the start, but he'd ignored his instincts.

He had thought it couldn't get any worse, but with Alexis Mission's arrival, the whole situation had gone from catastrophe to meltdown.

Pulling a radio from his vest, he spoke in an urgent voice, ordering a perimeter setup. He didn't have a lot of men, but those he had were the best. They'd give him as much time as they could.

Disconnecting, he considered the solutions one by

one, rejecting ideas as soon as they came to him. The Missions had told him about their daughter. They'd described her as smart and artistic, stubborn and head-strong. They'd emphasized the stubborn part. He had to keep that foremost in his mind.

Putting his weapon away, he searched the room with quick, efficient moves. She hadn't unpacked, thank God. He put away the towels and blanket that had been left on the bed, then he grabbed her duffel and went down the hall, checking the other rooms. As he worked, he felt the weight of what he carried in his pocket. The rings weren't heavy but his burden was.

Climbing into the Agency's helicopter a few hours before, Selena Mission had yanked off her wedding band and given it to him, turning to Robert and de-manding he do the same. "These are for Alexis," she'd said. "She can keep them until we see her again…"

Obeying his wife, Robert Mission had handed over his ring. The scientist had then gripped Gabriel's hand so hard, he'd left a mark that was still there. Selena hadn't accepted the truth yet, but the two men knew. The chances of the Missions ever seeing their daugh-ter again were nonexistent, especially if Gabriel was successful in his lies. And he'd better be. Everyone's lives—including hers—depended on it.

"If she doesn't show up—" Robert had said.

"I'll find her."

"And if she does..."

"I'll tell her."

"The story we agreed on." Robert's voice left no room for argument.

Gabriel had lied many times in his life, had a lot of regrets, too. He didn't want to add this one to the list, but he didn't think he had another choice. He asked the question anyway. "Look, are you sure this is—"

Mission shook his head violently, not even allowing him to finish. "It's the only way. She's smart but she's stubborn, too obstinate for her own damn good. If she has any inkling of the truth—any idea that we're still alive—she'll come looking for us, no matter how well you guys hide us. It won't matter." He paused. "You've got to stop her, otherwise she'll keep going until she finds us. And you know better than we do what that means..."

Robert Mission's voice had broken at that point. "She's...she's the best part of us, O'Rourke. Please...please make sure she's taken care of. Promise me you'll make sure she's—"

Gabriel had kept his expression stony but he'd nodded and given his word. Then he'd prayed the girl wouldn't show up.

Obviously his prayers hadn't been heard. Now he had to take care of business.

"I CAN'T LET YOU GO inside, ma'am, I'm sorry. This is a restricted area."

"But you don't understand! I'm looking for my

parents. I'm sure you know them—Robert and Selena Mission? They work here.''

The guard pulled his cap down over his eyes, the furry earflaps doing little to keep him warm. In the distance, Alexis's headlights shone on a fifteen-foot-high barbed wire fence, a low office building barely visible in the empty stretch of loneliness before her. Piñon trees with low twisted branches added their shadows to the scene. She stared at the facility in amazement. When had think tanks become equipped with security like this? The other places where her parents had worked had looked like college campuses.

The guard leaned down. "We're closed. No one's working here tonight."

"But do you know them? Have you seen them?"

He shook his head, his gloved fingers going to his jacket and pulling it closer. "I don't know anyone who works here. I man the gate when everyone else is off. I'm sorry I can't help you, but I have my instructions. You'll have to move along."

Alexis rolled up her window. There was nothing she could do but turn around and head back into town, her fear and frustration growing. She drove slower than before, the roads slicker and more dangerous than they'd been earlier, a thin layer of ice covering the highway. By the time she reached the house, she was a nervous wreck, her stomach in knots, her hands cramping against the steering wheel. She turned the

corner, praying she'd see lights, but the house was as
dark as she had left it. A wash of unbelievable disappointment came over her. Where in the world had
they gone?

She angled the car carefully into the driveway and
shut off the engine, sleet now pinging against the
metal roof in an uneasy rhythm. She didn't know
what to do other than try the police department again.
She should have filed a report earlier, but she hadn't
wanted to seem foolish. Looking silly was the last
thing she cared about now.

She gathered her purse, then opened the car door
and dashed to the front porch in the freezing night.
Fumbling with the keys she'd grabbed on the way out,
she found the right one, unlocked the dead bolt and
walked quickly into the entry.

For reasons she couldn't explain, the shadows inside seemed thicker than they had before, closer
somehow, pressing down against her and making it
tough to breathe. She wanted to call out but she knew
no one would answer, so she didn't bother. Her fingers found the light switch a second later and she
flipped it up. But nothing happened. Her mouth went
dry as she tried once more. The darkness remained,
indeed, seemed to increase.

She took a step into the living room then stopped
abruptly.

A man dressed completely in black sat in her father's chair. Alexis stared at him in shock, a sense of

dread coming over her with such intensity, she felt her entire body go hot, her blood turning to needles as it coursed through her veins. In the space of a heartbeat she was more scared than she'd ever been in her life. She couldn't move, couldn't talk, couldn't do anything but stare at the stranger. An aura of foreboding hung above him like a hangman's noose.

He looked at her through the gloom and spoke in a low voice. "You're Alexis."

Wishing she could answer another way, she nodded slowly.

"I'm Gabriel O'Rourke. I'm here to explain."

CHAPTER TWO

FROZEN IN PLACE, Alexis Mission stared at him, her eyes filling with fright. She was, he realized, trying to decide if she should scream, run or sit down and listen.

While she made up her mind, he took his own measure of her.

She wasn't at all what he'd expected.

The obstinacy and intelligence the Missions had told him about shone in the girl's eyes but they had said nothing about her appearance. She was beautiful...or was she? The shining brunette hair hung around a face with features that didn't mesh. The eyes were too big, the nose too straight. Her lips were too full as well. Taken one at a time, each component was attractive but she needed to age, he realized, for everything to fit.

Because she was young. Oh, God, she was so young...

Without any warning, she darted toward the phone. He jumped up but she punched two numbers before he could stop her, his fingers around her wrist, his face inches from hers.

She held on to the receiver and looked at him defiantly. Her attitude made him think of her mother. Selena had never let fear stop her, either.

"Take your hands off me and let go of the telephone," the girl said with determination.

He didn't answer—or release her.

They were standing close in the darkness, the skin beneath his fingers warm and smooth, her wrist bones fragile in his grip. He could have snapped them without any effort.

"What do you want?" she whispered. "Who are you?"

"I work for the government." He rattled off an acronym, but he knew it meant nothing to her. Robert and Selena wouldn't have told their daughter about him because that would have meant telling her about themselves. And they would *never* have done that.

Taking the phone away from her, he put it back in the cradle and dropped her arm. But he didn't step away.

She rubbed her wrist. "I want to see some ID."

"We don't have time for a dog and pony show. I have to get you out of here."

"Get me out of here... What on earth are you talking about?" She started shaking her head. "I'm not going anywhere with you—"

He reached inside the pocket of his jacket, pulled

out a leather wallet and flipped it open, handing it to her. She studied the card and the authentic-looking seal, comparing the photo to his face. The documentation meant nothing, but he carried it for people like her, people who kept their wits about them when he showed up. The Agency he worked for didn't hand out IDs or have a fancy office. It didn't even exist—at least not in a way that meant anything to others.

Looking unconvinced, she returned the credentials. "Where's my family? What have you done to them?"

The lie tasted bad and he cursed himself for what he was about to do. The girl's future held nothing but trouble, thanks to him. Along with confusion and anger. Grief and loneliness. He told himself again he didn't have a choice, but that knowledge didn't make the task any easier.

Plan your work and work your plan... His da would of been proud of him, he thought bitterly. *Never give up, never say die.* The old man had been full of useless clichés and he'd drilled every one of them into his sons—usually with a hard fist for punctuation—thinking they'd bring them the success that had always eluded him. His theory hadn't worked.

The girl made a sound of distress, breaking his thoughts.

"Relax," he said. "I haven't done anything to them and I'm not going to do anything to you, either. If I'd wanted to, I would have done it by now."

She moved back a step, away from him as much

as possible, her eyes wary, her body still poised to flee. "Where are they?"

"There's been a problem."

Her expression shifted. "Are they okay? What's happened? Where are—"

He interrupted her. "Your father saw something he shouldn't have this morning. He saw someone get killed. And the murderer saw your father…"

"A murder… Oh my God!" She lifted her fingers to her neck. At the base of her throat, a slim gold chain glistened. His eyes went to the tiny heart it held. All at once, in spite of her bravado, she seemed too vulnerable to Gabriel, too defenseless to handle what was coming next. "But Dad's okay, right? My family's—"

Before she could finish her sentence, she halfway turned to the door, then stopped in confusion and looked at him again, her eyes filled with worry. Cold had seeped into the house since he'd cut off the power and her words came out in quick bursts of vapor. "I should go to the police station. That's where they are, isn't it? I'd better—"

"No." Seeing his expression, finally sensing something, she stood still, his one-word answer hanging in the chilly living room between them.

He pointed to the couch. "Sit down."

Surprising him, she followed his command.

"You *can't* see them." He held her eyes in the darkness, his words slicing through the moment with the sharpness of a razor held to a throat. "They're dead." He waited a second. "They're gone. All of them."

She blinked against the pronouncement, her expression a study of misunderstanding. "I don't…" She shook her head slightly, her hair gleaming against the chenille upholstery of the sofa. She licked her lips and started over. "What do you mean, they're 'gone'? They can't just be 'gone.' They have to be somewhere—"

Gabriel wasn't sure why he moved to take her hand, but he did. Sitting down beside her, he reached out. Whatever his reason had been, though, it didn't matter. She snatched her fingers away before he could touch her. He spoke quietly. "The shooter killed them."

Unable to speak, she shook her head again, her fingers now spread across her open mouth.

"He couldn't leave anyone who might testify against him later."

"But Toby…Mother…"

"They were waiting for your father and saw what happened. The killer saw them, too."

Her eyes deepened to a darker color, denial her only defense. "No," she whispered, shaking her head again. "No. This…this can't be happening. I—I don't believe you…"

Reaching inside the pocket of his jacket, Gabriel

pulled out an envelope and handed it to her. Her fingers trembled as she unfolded the flap.

A moment later, she looked up from the wedding bands, her eyes so similar to her father's, they threw Gabriel for a moment. "Th-this doesn't prove anything. Y-you could have stolen them, for all I know."

"I didn't steal the rings. I had them with me because I was going to mail them to you later." He paused. "I assumed your mother would have wanted you to have them."

The girl's reaction was a living thing; it sucked the air from the room and then from him. Gabriel fought the sensation and overcame it, but not without a struggle, which surprised him. He puzzled for a moment over why. Maybe it was the way she looked or maybe her youth. Either way, he didn't know and he didn't care. He *couldn't* care.

"We have to leave." He glanced at his watch then stood. Looking down at her, he came as close to the truth as he had all night. "The man your father saw— he's associated with some very bad people. If they figure out you exist, they're going to come after you, too. They won't quit until they find you, and after they've used you up, they'll kill you. If I can get you out of Los Lobos quickly enough and under some kind of protection, that *might* not happen." He paused. "Emphasis on 'might.'"

Alexis stared at him, her gaze so pointed it made him uneasy. "That doesn't make sense. If my family was killed because they witnessed a murder, why would the killer—or anyone associated with him—come after me? I didn't see anything.''

Gabriel wasn't surprised she could analyze the situation while mired in grief. Robert had told him the truth.

''It doesn't make sense,'' she insisted.

''Of course it doesn't make sense.'' Gabriel made his voice harsh. ''Do you think the baby could identify him?'' He didn't wait for her reply because he wasn't going to get one—he'd shocked her, and that was exactly why he'd spoken as he had. ''This man is a killer. He *enjoys* it. The people he surrounds himself with enjoy it, too. Killing is entertainment for them.''

Devastated by his words, she sat on the sofa, stunned and silent. The expression on her face made Gabriel feel ill but he ignored the sensation. ''If you hadn't shown up, this might not have been a problem, but you did, so now we have to deal with it. That's why I'm here.''

Without waiting for her to reply, Gabriel moved toward the window. A car moved slowly down the street. Relatives looking for a holiday gathering or something else? His jaw tensed and the rest of his body followed. He turned away from the glass, a new urgency coming into his voice. ''Get up and get ready. It's time to leave.''

The speed of her movement took him so off guard,

he automatically reached behind him, toward the .38.
She flew at him, her hands clawing at his face.

"You're lying to me!" she screamed. "You did
something to them yourself! You're the one who
killed them!"

He gripped her arms and forced them down, slapping his fingers over her mouth to cut off her words
before they had the chance to go any further. Above
his hand, her eyes were huge.

"I *did not* kill your family," he growled. "Why
would I stick around here and wait for you to show
up then tell you what I'd done? Does that even sound
remotely logical?"

Instead of answering, she tried again to scream. He
squeezed her jaw with the barest of force, shaking her
slightly. "You don't want to do this," he warned.
"You don't want to make problems for me. Do you
understand?"

Her body trembled, vibrated, in fact, like a string
on a violin that had been drawn too roughly. Finally
she blinked, then blinked again. He took that for a
reply, but he didn't remove his hand as he spoke.

"Problems for me mean problems for you. You do
not—I repeat—*do not* want anyone to know you even
came here tonight. Your flight records have already
been erased and the car you came in is gone. I had it
moved the minute you stepped inside here." He took
a deep breath, her scent reaching him before he could
ignore it. "Do you understand what I'm telling you?"

This time he did ease his fingers, but he didn't take away his hand. She started to speak, her mouth moving against the inside of his palm, sending a sensation into his gut.

"I called the police—"

"No, you didn't," he said.

It took her a stunned second to understand. "But I went to the center. I talked to the guard—"

He removed his hand, but kept his grip on her arm. "He's been taken care of. Did you talk to anyone else, see anyone?"

"No…I…" She looked dazed, almost as if she was slipping into shock, her touch with reality slipping as well. "Ju-just the neighbors…" she said with distraction.

"They've been dealt with, too." Locking his stare on hers, he spoke again. "Now all we have to do is take care of you…"

NUMB WITH DISBELIEF, Alexis watched the man gather up her things. He worked quickly and efficiently—he'd done this kind of thing before. Glancing into the dining room from the living room where she stood, she saw that he'd already removed the extra place setting from the table. If she bothered to look, she was sure she'd see that the linens in her bedroom were back in the closet as well. Within moments, he was finished. Glancing down at her watch, she was shocked by how quickly the minutes passed since she'd come back into the house.

He walked into the kitchen. She lifted her eyes to his face but she already had the details memorized; she could live to be a hundred and she'd never forget what he looked like. Wolfish eyes and thick black hair. Broad shoulders and a muscular body. A square jaw. A cruel mouth.

Cold. Stony. Callous.

His voice was clipped, his demeanor unreadable. Alexis had a fine ear for languages and she'd recognized the barest hint of an accent, something British, maybe Irish.

"It's time." The burr sounded again. "Let's go."

"Where—"

"Where doesn't matter!" Until this point, his total calm had been almost eerie, his attitude colder than she could comprehend. Now she heard frustration, got a hint of anger.

He took a step toward her. "Don't you get it? I've *got* to remove you and we've taken way too long already." He jerked a thumb toward the street. "I can't guarantee what's going to happen if we don't get out of here and soon."

He headed toward the back door then turned when she didn't follow. His eyes bored a painful path into her. "Don't do this," he warned.

Alexis shuffled toward him, her legs weak, her brain whirling with all the questions she had. How did she know this man was who he said he was? She certainly hadn't recognized the badge or the name of his agency. And his story... God, it was crazy! She could be walking straight into something horrible instead of fleeing danger. Grief and terror mixed inside her with confusion and alarm. What should she do?

Her panic blossomed. She picked up the photo she'd looked at earlier. Then she tensed her body, pivoted and ran straight for the front door.

Her fingertips were brushing the doorknob when he grabbed her from behind.

"What in the hell do you think you're doing?" He twisted her around to face him, his breath hot against her cheeks. "Are you crazy? Do you *want* to die?"

"Let me go." She pushed at his hands, but for all the good it did, she shouldn't have bothered. His fingers were steel bars wrapped around her arms. "I don't want to leave. I don't want—"

"Good God Almighty! I thought you were bright." He shook her slightly, his tone so toxic she stopped her protests. His grip tightened. "Your father told me you had your mother's brains. Was the poor man daft or was he lying to me?"

Alexis froze. Her father *had* teased her with those words a million times, his smile as wide as the gold band on his finger, the wedding band he, just like her mother, never removed. Ever.

One by one, the details added up and Alexis's heart sank from the weight of them.

The man read her reaction immediately. He jerked the small frame from her fingers and stuffed it into his coat pocket. Then he turned and headed for the back door, yanking Alexis along behind him.

GABRIEL PICKED a no-name motel on the edge of the interstate three hours away. The place was run-down and deserted, which was exactly why he'd picked it. Paying cash, he then drove the van to the last room at the back of the low concrete-block building and parked, turning to look at Alexis as he switched off the engine. She was sitting on the floor of the vehicle and barely seemed aware of where they were. Her entire life had just been turned upside down and he was the one shaking the globe. If she ever found out the truth, the glimpses of resistance he'd witnessed earlier would pale in comparison to what would follow.

He pushed his thoughts aside and climbed out of the van. With one hand on his weapon, he let his eyes sweep the parking lot. As they'd escaped through the back of the Missions' house to the van, he'd thought he'd heard a car drive by the front, but his men had told him to leave and he had, without looking back. He studied the empty blacktop before him now, then he twisted the door handle and reached inside. "Let's go."

She didn't resist. Climbing out of the vehicle without a word, she walked beside him to the door of their room. The fact that his hand was wrapped around her upper arm assured her cooperation. He kept a steady hold on her until they stepped inside and he'd thrown the lock behind them.

The tiny room was clean, but that was all Gabriel could say about it. A small table in one corner was propped up by a telephone book, its lamp askew, the chair beside it worn and threadbare. Gabriel knew nothing about decorating, but the last time he'd seen a spread like the one stretched over the sagging bed, the year had been 1970-something.

He strode toward the bathroom and flipped on the light. A harsh fluorescence lit the room. He checked behind the shower curtain, then made the mistake of glancing into the mirror.

He'd aged ten years in the past forty-eight hours.

His skin was the pasty color of an old man's, his hair spiky and dark. A black shadow covered his jawline and circles of exhaustion hung under his eyes. He scrubbed his face with his hands and looked again. God in heaven, no wonder Alexis Mission had been scared of him. He scared himself.

A sudden squeak sounded in the room behind him. His hand on his weapon, Gabriel pivoted and pushed through the door...then he relaxed. Alexis had lain down, the box springs so worn they creaked under even her slight weight. Walking over to the bed, he studied her but her expression was blank when she looked up at him.

"Are you hungry?" He glanced over his shoulder

to the parking lot beyond the window. "I've got some stuff in the van if you are."

She stared at him for a moment, then without a word she rolled over and faced the wall.

He stood silent and still. For now, she'd shut down, her emotions and reactions too raw and exposed for her to even comprehend, but later she'd have more questions. He'd seen it happen before. Gabriel turned to the chair in the corner and dragged it to the door with one hand. Propping it under the knob, he sat down wearily, his body unsteady, his mind drained. He wished he could sleep but knew he couldn't.

A long time would come and go before he could experience that luxury again.

ALEXIS CLUTCHED her paper coffee cup, the steam rising slowly between her face and Gabriel O'Rourke's. They were sitting inside the van, somewhere off the main highway, exactly where she had no idea. He'd woken her after what felt like only a few hours' sleep, and they'd gotten into the vehicle, driving for a full hour before he was satisfied enough to stop and get them coffee from a run-down all-night diner. She wasn't too sure what he was doing, but she suspected he was checking to see if they were being followed. The knowledge didn't make her feel any better. Neither had waking up and realizing he'd been watching her as she'd slept.

He was trying his best to fool her, but she was sure the man sitting in front of her knew more than he was letting on. She swallowed the pain and confusion that filled her. "Who do you work for, again?"

"You've already asked me that and I've answered it. Asking me again is not going to get you a different response." A lock of dark hair fell down on his forehead before he pushed it back impatiently. "It doesn't matter anyway. All I'm here to do is make sure you understand what *has* happened and what's *going* to happen next."

Despite everything he'd said, she couldn't accept— didn't want to accept—what he'd told her. It wasn't possible, she kept telling herself. "I—I can't just walk away like this. No funeral. No services. It's not right."

His glance went to the deserted highway that ran beside them, exactly as it had at least a dozen times while they'd been sitting there drinking coffee. When his eyes came back to Alexis, they held a different kind of darkness from before, and she trembled, despite herself.

"I thought you understood." He leaned closer, his manner hard and impatient. "I don't know how to say it any other way than I've already said it a thousand times. You *can't* see the bodies or bury them. It would take too much time. In fact, we've already… taken care of that." He held out his hands almost in defeat, the first gesture he'd made that seemed human to her. "I'm sorry, Alexis, but they're gone." He shook his head. *"They are gone."*

She wasn't sure if it was his voice or the use of

her name, but all at once his words sunk in, the reality of what they actually meant ripping into her with a force that tore her breath away. The last vestige of her denial was destroyed along with it.

"They're dead," she whispered.

He nodded, a tinge of something that looked like pity crossing his expression before he could prevent its appearance.

"Toby's only four," she said inexplicably.

"He *was* four."

His use of the past tense didn't escape her, but Alexis refused to let herself cry. She wouldn't let him see her do that. It took everything she had, but she composed herself, then looked up. Gabriel O'Rourke stared back. His eyes held the total force of his intensity and it was directed straight at her.

"You *cannot* go back to Los Lobos. Ever. You understand that, don't you?"

"Yes," she said numbly.

"The house will be sold. The proceeds will go into a bank account and they'll be forwarded to you. Everything else—any other accounts they might have held—will be sent to you later." He crumpled his coffee cup and dropped it to the floorboard of the van. "I'm going to put you on a plane in a bit and you'll fly away from here. People will meet you at the other end. They'll take care of you."

"What does that mean?"

"You'll get a new life."

"A new life? I don't want a new life. I want my old one back."

"That's impossible. It's gone."

"That easily?" She snapped her fingers, her voice breaking. "You can erase people's existence just like that? Their history? Their lives? Everything they are? You have that much power?"

He ignored the question. "After this, you're going to be someone else. My organization doesn't put people into the Witness Protection Program but they *will* help you. You'll get a new home and a new name—"

She laughed, an edge of hysteria accompanying the sound. "Do I get a new family, too? A new mom and dad? How about a baby brother? Can we add a little sister, too?"

He didn't react at all. He simply stared at her, those bottomless black eyes taking it all in without a flicker.

She blinked and looked away, the finality hitting her again, harder than ever. She thought of a thousand things she wished she'd grabbed from the house. Her mother's fake pearls. The video of her graduation. Toby's Pooh bear. Her father's favorite sweater. None of it valuable but all of it priceless. Then she thought of the photo. When Gabriel O'Rourke had ripped that picture from her hands, he'd taken her history as well. Her past was gone. Her family was gone.

She was gone. The person she'd been twenty-four hours ago no longer existed.

And she had a bad feeling that she didn't even

know the real reason behind the nightmare. "Why?" she said almost to herself. "Why?"

Surprising her, the man in black answered her question, his voice a knife. "Your father was an honorable man, that's why. He always did the right thing."

"And Mom?"

He shrugged, the emotion he'd allowed her to see already evaporating, already disappearing. "She loved him." He paused. "Just like they both loved you. That's one thing that's for certain."

"Nothing's for certain." Alexis looked down, into her coffee mug. An oily reflection of her face looked back, more real to her right now than her actual existence. She lifted her eyes. "Not anymore. You've taken that away from me."

"But you have your life," he answered. "And you will be safe. I'll see to that."

She tried to doubt him but she couldn't. For the first time since they'd met, she knew Gabriel O'Rourke was telling her the truth.

HE TOOK HER to a small private airstrip, three hours away from where they'd been. They didn't speak the whole trip, both occupied with their own thoughts and regrets. He'd let her ride in the passenger seat after they'd finished their coffee, his fears growing dimmer with each mile he put between the house on the quiet street and them. When they arrived and he'd parked, Gabriel turned to the young woman beside him.

He thought he'd aged, but Alexis Mission now looked like an entirely different person. Part of the change was at his insistence. They'd stopped at a twenty-four-hour drugstore and gotten a bottle of bleach and some harsh makeup. In a service-station bathroom near the interstate, the brunette he'd grabbed inside the Mission home had become a blonde with a slash of red lipstick that didn't match her skin tone.

The changes to Alexis Mission went beyond just the physical, though. Her eyes were completely empty, her demeanor that of another person. She was someone less sure, he decided. Someone less confident, the darkness of depression already settling into her soul.

A small Cessna taxied out of a rusted hangar to their right and headed to where they were parked. Behind the plane, the tips of the mountains were just beginning to glow in the rising sun's rays. Gabriel handed Alexis an envelope and she took it woodenly, placing it in her lap.

"There's some cash in there to get you by until the money is wired. My people at the other end will give you more." He held out a small white card and she took it, too. "That's how you can reach me. It's a drop number."

She looked at him impassively.

"You call it and leave a message," he explained. "Then I phone you back. You won't ever get me directly. The system doesn't work that way."

Her eyes went to the piece of paper with the phone number written on it. She stared at it for a moment then she crumpled the note into a ball and opened her fingers. It fell to the floorboards.

"You might need that," he said softly.

"I don't think so," she said. "You've done enough already."

Her stiff reply wasn't a compliment. Alexis Mission held him accountable for everything that had happened because she had no one else to blame. Similar damnation had been heaped on him before.

But he hadn't cared then.

He felt the need to say something. "Alexis, your family was... Your mom and dad..."

"Don't bother," she said. The swosh of the plane's rotors drawing close, she opened the van's door, a wave of frigid air sweeping into the vehicle as she stepped out. She spoke through the window, her fingers gripping the edge so tightly her knuckles went white. "I don't want to hear whatever you're trying to say to me. I've had enough of your lies to last me forever."

Her glittering gaze met with his, then she turned and walked away.

CHAPTER THREE

Ten years later, Austin, Texas

ALEX WORTHINGTON dusted off the last table in her workroom and picked up an errant paintbrush that had escaped her notice. Tucking the brush into a nearby drawer, she surveyed the area one more time. When Claiborne Academy's final bell rang at Thanksgiving break, most of the staff fled as quickly as the students, but not Alex. She liked to return in January to a tidy space and a fresh start.

Fresh starts were her specialty. She'd had quite a few of them.

Claiborne itself represented one of the better ones. Alex had been the school's resident artist for almost four years, her longest stretch anywhere. A private facility, the exclusive Austin school that blended art and technology was the favorite of parents who had plenty of money and wanted to spend it on their kids. When they'd hired her, she'd warned the administrators she wasn't a teacher and they'd said they weren't looking for one. Claiborne was innovative—the facility needed someone who would "guide" the children into developing their own creativeness, not teach them.

Atypical in its schedule as well as its philosophy, the academy shut down completely between Thanksgiving and New Year's so the students and their families could head across the globe to second homes and exotic vacations. The faculty escaped as best they could and collapsed...working at Claiborne demanded a lot.

Alex was different though. She didn't mind the hours any more than she minded tidying up her area, especially at this time of year. For obvious reasons, the holiday stretch always left her feeling restless and anxious. She usually planned an out-of-the-way trip herself, but before she could make reservations this year, Ben had called.

They'd married six years ago. After two, they'd divorced but had remained really good friends. Ben had asked her to spend Christmas with him and Libby, his twenty-year-old daughter. Alex couldn't turn him down. Twenty-five years her senior, Ben was dying from a rare liver disease and he wouldn't see another Christmas. If he wanted Alex with him, then she had to go. She owed him that much...and probably a lot more.

Taking down the last of the few decorations she put up each year—a gathered stalk of dried corn and apples—she told herself she'd get through tomorrow, then concentrate on Ben and Libby. They each needed Alex in a different way, and helping them would take her mind off her memories and all the ghosts that came with them.

But just thinking about the past summoned everything to her. Her fingers suddenly tightened on the dried corn husks and pieces of the chaff fluttered to the floor. She stared at the yellow bits, then all at once, despite her best intentions, her heart started to pound and her mouth went dry. With a quiet groan, she closed her eyes. Behind the lids, the image of her mother's wreath appeared. The lopsided arrangement looked just as it had on the door of the house in Los Lobos the day Alex had come home from Peru.

Gabriel O'Rourke's face came next, but before it could fully form, a voice broke the silence.

"Hey, you're supposed to go home first and then fall asleep!"

Alex's eyes shot open. Randy Squires, Claiborne's dean, stood in the doorway of her classroom and grinned.

She smiled gratefully at the tall, balding man. Randy was a sweetheart and he never failed to make her feel better, no matter how badly the day had gone. If she let him, she suspected he'd give his right arm to make her happy, although he'd never come out and asked her for a date or made any kind of obvious move. He was too professional for that, but even more importantly, he sensed the wall Alex kept around herself and respected it.

"I'm too tired to go home and go to bed," she lied. "I think I'll just hibernate here like some big old bear until January. Is that okay?"

He strolled into her classroom and perched on the edge of her desk. "No fancy trips this year? No big vacation?"

Alex shook her head and explained Ben's situation.

"I'm sorry to hear he's so ill."

"I am, too." She sat down at one of the tables in front of her desk. "Ben's a nice guy."

"Your divorce was amicable, I take it?"

"Very. The last thing Ben Worthington would do is make a fuss over a divorce. He's too much of a gentleman."

"But the marriage didn't work?"

Alex didn't discuss anything personal with anyone. She couldn't. "No," she said in a curt voice. "It didn't work."

Her sharpness brought him to his feet. "I guess I'd better head home. If you get bored during the break, give me a call. There's a new Mexican place over on Guadalupe Street. We could hit it."

Alex felt a sweep of guilt—she shouldn't have been so harsh—but she kept her face noncommittal. "Sure." She nodded. "I'll keep that in mind. It sounds like a lot of fun."

Then their eyes met and both of them knew she wouldn't call.

He left a few minutes after that. Relief washed over Alex as she picked up her purse and briefcase to follow his path out the door. Randy was the kind of guy any woman would be thrilled to have. Any woman but Alex.

She didn't want anyone in her life, so it was always

best to head off relationships before they started: You never knew when the other person might up and disappear.

GABRIEL O'ROURKE watched the bartender flick his rag at the caged parrot hanging over the bar. The sight provided the most entertainment Gabriel had had in the past two days. There wasn't much to do in Baja this time of year. Or any time of year, but that was exactly why Gabriel came here, or so he told himself.

He'd left the Agency the year before, and he hadn't given a damn about anything during that time. Caring cost more than he had to give, emotionally and physically. Burned out and disillusioned, when he needed money he did contract work for the government.

He took a sip of his lukewarm Dos Equis and listened to the conversation of the people sitting behind him in the bar. They'd come in late last night, two couples from Denver. The men had talked incessantly about fishing, but Gabriel had the feeling they'd already been hooked. One blonde, one redhead, the women were much younger than the men and their jewelry outshone the lights above the bar. Gabriel wondered idly if the men's wives knew where they were.

"Well, pecan is my favorite." One of the women behind him spoke in a deep Southern accent, the words drifting over Gabriel's shoulder along with cigar smoke from the man at her side. Gabriel glanced at her in the mirror above the bar—it was the blonde.

"We always had it on the table when I was growing up. It's just not Thanksgiving without pecan pie."

The redhead said something, the men guffawing at her reply, but Gabriel didn't hear her. His brain was still trying to absorb what the first woman had said.

Until that very moment, he hadn't realized tomorrow would be Thanksgiving.

A shadow glided across his memory, the whisper of a young woman with a pale face and stunned expression. He blinked and tried to send her away, but he failed as always. Standing up, he threw a handful of pesos on the bar and left, the cool breeze from the ocean hitting his face as he walked outside.

The ghost of Alexis Mission followed him.

Opening the screen door to his bungalow, Gabriel stepped inside the one-room shack. He grabbed another beer from a cooler he kept stocked, then he turned and went back outside to the porch. Fifteen yards away the Pacific Ocean rolled endlessly, the sky beyond it so dark and deep it made him dizzy just to look at it. He'd been on the sandy strip of beach for a week, his original reason for coming the same as the men in the bar—the fishing. He had yet to rent a boat though, and when he was honest with himself, he knew he probably wouldn't. He'd come to Baja to recuperate, not to fish.

The month before, he'd finished another job for the Agency…and another relationship, and he'd wanted somewhere private to lick his wounds. Usually he missed the former more than the latter, but this time had been different.

He'd met the woman in a bar and Gabriel had been shocked when she'd come to his table and sat down to strike up a conversation. Like men everywhere, he'd kept his mouth shut and let her do her thing, his ego inflating with each admiring glance she'd sent his way. She'd been beautiful and smart and ambitious. Younger than him, too, a *helluva* lot younger, but then again…weren't they all?

She'd moved *in* two weeks later and *out* after two months. He'd packed up his shit and left San Diego. It wasn't home anyway—no place was home. He'd come down here.

And now it was almost Thanksgiving.

Gabriel stared at the water but Alexis Mission's face formed in the waves and mocked him. Like still photos framed inside his mind, he saw snapshots of her life, times when he'd been there and she'd never known. The rough period right after Los Lobos. The emergency room, then the recuperation. The paintings. Her wedding. The divorce. Her job. Each event had brought him close to her…but never *too* close.

Gabriel had told so many lies in his work he couldn't remember them all, but he'd never forgotten the ones he'd told Alexis Mission.

Back then, though, catching Guy Cuvier had been his only goal. The man had gotten away with stealing American technology for years and Gabriel had been so determined to stop him that nothing else had mattered. The result had been disastrous and the deception still haunted him: Alexis Mission's parents hadn't been killed. And Richard Mission hadn't witnessed a murder.

He'd committed one.

It'd been self-defense, of course, but Richard had shot Guy Cuvier. Gabriel had worked quickly, knowing nothing but a total disappearance could keep the Missions safe afterward. He'd been wrong about that and regretted the decision as much as he now regretted telling Alexis that her family had died. The idea had seemed like a bad one at the time; in retrospect, it was the *worst* thing Gabriel could have done.

In the past few years, it seemed as if things had begun to smooth out for Alexis. The new name had become her own, the town her home, the life, one she liked. Deep down, however, Gabriel often wondered if her adjustment was genuine. In his eyes, she wore her past like a mask she couldn't take off. The divorce had set her back, too. Before she'd even married the guy, Gabriel had predicted the outcome. Ben Worthington had been too old for Alexis. He was incapable of giving her what she searched for, what she needed.

Truth be told, Gabriel had actually thought at one point about making contact with her, but he'd held back. Why disrupt her life a second time? Six months after Los Lobos, part of the lie he'd told her had actually come to pass, but there was no good reason to revive her sorrow. She'd already grieved for her parents and brother—unearthing an empty grave just to dig a real one was too cruel to even consider. Gabriel carried enough guilt as it was.

He told himself she wouldn't have listened to him, anyway. Before leaving the cold mountains outside of Los Lobos, Alexis Mission had made herself perfectly clear; he was the last person on earth she ever wanted to see again. She hated him.

Gabriel hadn't felt the same way about her. He'd made a promise to watch over her, but for the past ten years that pledge had meant nothing to him.

He'd kept vigil over Alexis Mission because he couldn't stay away.

THEY SAID they heated the pool, but the water still felt icy to Alex. She stuck her big toe into the deep end and tried not to think about it, choosing instead to simply dive in and swim. As it was with most things, that seemed to be the best policy. With even, steady strokes she sliced through the water and quickly reached the other end. Touching the cold tile with her fingertips, she sucked in a breath then flipped over to head back the way she had just come.

The natatorium wasn't usually empty but it might as well have been tonight. Only two other swimmers occupied the lanes to either side, their strokes splashing loud enough to keep her company. Everyone was sleeping off their Thanksgiving feasts; going to the YMCA was the last thing on their minds.

In general, Alex liked it when no one else was around and she was the only one in the water. Tonight, though, she welcomed the other swimmers. There was something creepy about the echoing walls, something unnerving about the size of the room.

She was nervous and edgy, more behind her anxiety than just the holidays: For the past few days she'd been sure someone was following her. Every time she'd stepped outside her apartment, she'd experienced the horrible sensation of eyes on her back. Her neck would tingle and she'd look around sharply, but so far she'd spotted no one. The feeling refused to leave, however.

Thrusting these thoughts away, she swam for almost forty minutes, her arms and legs growing heavy toward the end. A half-hour workout was her usual maximum, but tonight she wanted to tire herself out completely. She finished the final lap then clung to the edge of the pool and fought to regain her breath. When her huffing and puffing slowed and she looked around, she realized everyone else had left. She was all alone.

Paddling quickly to the edge of the pool, Alex climbed out and grabbed the towel she'd draped over a chair. She made her way to the ladies' locker room and within fifteen minutes, she'd showered and dressed and was on her way to the parking lot.

The day had been a repeat of Alex's other Thanksgivings. Over the years, she'd developed a finely tuned ritual, a way she both remembered then walked away from her past. The rite was never completely successful of course, but one day it might be. One day she *might* find herself unable to recall every single detail.

As she always did, she'd started the morning by writing a letter to Toby. There were ten of the white envelopes now, sitting in a box, just waiting. He would never read the letters, of course, but they weren't for her little brother anyway. They were for her. She didn't want to forget him. When she finished that task, she sat back and closed her eyes. The memories she kept tightly guarded the rest of the year were then allowed out.

The empty house. The icy road. The look on Gabriel O'Rourke's face when he'd told her her family was dead. As soon as she could, rendering the images with sharp, swift strokes, Alexis had re-created the photo that he'd ripped from her hands that night. Holding that sketch, she sat in the middle of her bed and let the past flood her. At first, the ritual had almost killed her, but lately, the mental pictures had begun to dim. If she hadn't had her charcoal memory, her mother's eyes would be a blur now, her father's expression a dim relief. Alex wasn't sure if this was good or bad.

She immersed herself in the pain for an hour and then she stopped. The ghosts went back into the lockbox she kept inside her heart. The framed drawing returned to its position on her nightstand and she forced herself through the day.

The YMCA had been a last-minute addition to her routine. Because of her anxiety about being followed, the ritual hadn't cooperated and the past kept breaking in, flashes of the night she wanted to forget coming back. Reaching her car, Alex knew she'd have to think of something else to do to keep it all at bay. She'd pick up some movies, she decided impulsively, throwing her gym bag into the car and starting it. Something that would keep her mind more occupied than the book she'd been saving for that evening.

She stopped at the video store down the road from her apartment and grabbed two mindless films. The Thai place next door was open, so she went in there as well and ordered takeout. By the time she reached home, she'd managed to kill another hour. Glancing down at her watch, she figured she only had four more hours to endure. She'd allow herself a single sleeping pill then hopefully wake up to a day with fewer memories.

The parking lot of her apartment was almost as empty as the YMCA's pool had been. The complex was a small one near the University of Texas campus and a lot of the university people lived there. Students and professors alike, they were a transient bunch, coming and going with each semester, a fast turnover of neighbors who fled during the holidays and summer. Some people wouldn't have liked it for that very reason, but that was exactly why Alex had selected the apartment. She didn't want long-term neighbors who had to know your life's history. When you didn't have one you could talk about, conversation turned stilted.

Tonight, though, just like at the pool, she would have welcomed a few more souls. The hollow echo of her tennis shoes slapping the sidewalk was too reminiscent, the cold too chilling, the empty feeling too familiar. She had friends she could have called, other teachers, people from church... A number of them had even invited her to their homes for the holiday meal, but she'd turned down all the offers as she always did at Thanksgiving. She *needed* to be lonely on Thanksgiving.

But knowing this didn't diminish the emotion. Or the feelings of being frightened that were mixed with the loneliness. She ordered herself to buck up. She'd get through this year just as she had the other nine. By sheer grit and determination.

Alex climbed the stairs to her second-floor landing, then shifted the gym bag and the two plastic sacks to her left hand so she could unlock her door. Stepping inside, she closed the door behind her and locked it once more.

Then she froze.

Something wasn't right.

Someone had been inside her apartment.

Her glance shot to her right, into the well-lit living room. Her apartment was close to the pool and the lights from the patio came through her blinds at night. Bright lines sifted their way through the open slats to reveal the sofa and two chairs. They were empty. To her left, behind a wall, was a small kitchen.

Alex carefully emptied her arms, the sacks going to the floor, her gym bag dropping silently to a nearby table. With her eyes still sweeping the room in front of her, she felt behind her for the bat she kept by the front door. Gripping the taped handle with both hands, she advanced into the entry, her back to the wall, and lifted the bat to her shoulder as she stepped around the wall.

The kitchen was as empty as it had been when she'd left.

Her pulse ringing, Alex returned to the hallway that led to the guest bedroom. The room served as her studio and was filled with art equipment, a worktable and a potter's wheel, a small loom and drawing supplies. As she eased around the doorway, her eyes jerked to one corner, her heart stopping with a violent thump. A tall shadow was poised by the window. A second later, her scream died in her throat.

She was looking at her easel.

Sick with fright, she returned to the corridor and forced herself to continue. The guest bath was empty, too. The only rooms left were her bedroom and bath.

She crept toward the back of the apartment, her palms so wet her grip on the bat was slipping. Suddenly she wished she hadn't done the extra laps at the pool. The polished piece of oak felt as if it weighed fifty pounds. She wasn't sure she could swing it if she had to.

But her bedroom was just as empty as the rest of the place, the white matelassé bedspread smooth and pristine, her slippers tossed carelessly beside the bed, her robe in the chair on the right. Her chest eased slightly, her fear starting to fade.

It wouldn't have been the first time on Thanksgiving that she'd imagined the presence of another person in her home.

Her bathroom was as empty as the rest of the place. She was alone and no one had been in her apartment. The day had gotten to her, that's all. Her imagination—and her memories—were conjuring ghosts.

Her shoulders slumped and Alex leaned weakly against the tiled wall, taking a deep breath. Then the heat came on, and all at once she caught a whiff of gardenias. Her mother's favorite fragrance.

Alex knew what she smelled wasn't really there—it couldn't be—but her body went cold, her blood refusing to go through her veins. She held her breath for as long as she could, then she slowly released it and inhaled again. The scent was gone.

Letting the bat slip from her fingers, she waited for her heart to slow, the beats gradually subsiding from a pounding rhythm to a steady pulse. After a bit, she looked into the bathroom mirror and shook her head at what she saw. Her face was an oval of white, her expression frightened and anxious. She lifted her hands and nervously fingered her hair, the strands still limp and damp from her shower at the pool.

Returning to the living room, she sent her glance to the corner of the room. For years, she'd had nightmares after Los Lobos. She dreamed the same thing each time; she'd come home, unlock the door, and there would be a man waiting in the living room. Grabbing her by the arms, he would pull her toward the wall, then the wall would disappear, a huge hole replacing it. Looking straight into her eyes, he would pitch her into the darkness. Before she hit the bottom, she always woke up, shaking and screaming.

The man was faceless. But she knew who he was.

Turning abruptly, she went into the kitchen. She

grabbed a plate from the cabinet above the sink and dumped the container of pad thai into its center, sticking it into the microwave and punching the buttons with a trembling finger. She forced her mind into a blank state that didn't allow for any thinking.

Hours later, she woke up on the couch, her neck stiff from the hard cushions, her legs cramped. The clock read one-thirty, her dirty dishes were spread across the coffee table and the movie she'd rented had stopped on the DVD. She stumbled to her feet and thought about cleaning up, then rejected the idea. The mess would be fine until morning—she didn't want to wake up enough to deal with it. Her mind would grab the opportunity to go into high gear again and she'd never get back to sleep.

Feeling her way to the bedroom, Alex peeled off her clothes and dropped them at the foot of her bed, reaching for the nightgown she'd left on the chair. Her eyes half-closed, she found the silky garment and slipped it over her head. She didn't bother to wash her face or brush her hair. She simply yanked back the covers and fell into bed, her gaze flicking automatically toward the frame on her bedside table. Looking at those long-ago lost faces was the last thing she did every night and the first thing she did every morning.

She blinked once, then once again, her groggy brain not understanding the message her eyes had just sent. Finally, she reached out with a trembling hand and turned on the bedside lamp.

The nightstand was empty. Her sketch was gone.

CHAPTER FOUR

PARALYZED BY WHAT she didn't see, Alex held her breath and tried to understand. She was sure the drawing had been there that morning. She distinctly remembered sitting in the bed and holding it in her hands, staring at it, in fact.

Had she dropped it? Knocked it off the table? Put it somewhere else? Her heart lurched as she recalled the perfume she'd thought she'd smelled earlier, but she instantly pushed the idea aside. She was crazy to even think about it. Her mother was dead.

Throwing off the covers, Alex fell from the bed to the floor where she began to search. Looking around to the back of the table and then underneath the bed frame, she found nothing but dust balls. No glint of silver, no paper with charcoal smudges...nothing.

She jumped to her feet and ran into the bathroom. The countertop was as uncluttered as always, a box of tissues and her makeup bag taking up one corner, her toothbrush, a can of hair spray and some jewelry clustered at the other end. Feeling foolish, she drew back the shower curtain. The empty tub gleamed.

Her consternation grew, but as Alex made a quick circuit of the apartment, she realized the rooms were exactly as she had left them when she'd gone to sleep on the sofa. Not a thing had been touched, not even the cash she kept in a jar in the kitchen for emergencies. Nothing was missing. Except for the sketch.

Panic swept over her. She fought the crushing weight, but it was stronger than she was and all at once she couldn't breathe. Nausea came with the suffocation. She clawed at her throat, then gave up. Half running, half stumbling, she made it into the living room and grabbed the phone at the end of the couch.

She meant to dial 911, but her fingers punched out a different number. It was already ringing when she realized what she'd done.

"SEÑOR! Señor Bradford..."

Gabriel halted his unsteady progress across the hotel lobby as the clerk behind the counter called out his current alias. Sunburned, cranky and more than halfway tanked, Gabriel had actually gone fishing late that afternoon. By the time he and his guide had cleaned their catch, cooked it and finished the beer, midnight had come and gone. Glancing to where the clerk stood, Gabriel decided to blow him off. Then he looked at the man's face. He wore such an anxious expression Gabriel immediately changed course and went straight to the desk.

"You have a message." The clerk reached behind

the counter. "Several of them. A woman has been calling you more than one times. She did not believe me when I told her you weren't here. It is not good news, *señor*. You have my condolences..."

A ripple of unease went down Gabriel's spine and the bit of buzz he'd had left instantly.

Without a word, he took the pink message slips from the clerk. There were three of them and they each had the same message.

Grandmother has died. Call home immediately. Your loving sister, Samantha.

Gabriel stared at the writing and willed the words away, but when he looked again, they hadn't disappeared. He had no sisters by that name or any other. His grandmother had been dead and gone for twenty-five years, his father for five. His mom had disappeared when he was seven and no one had seen or heard from her since.

This message was from his drop number. Someone had called him.

With the clerk's repeated sympathies still ringing in the lobby, Gabriel made his way to his bungalow. He never left the country without calling the Agency and giving them his itinerary. It was a good thing old habits die hard, he guessed, his heart beating against his ribs.

Once inside, he went straight for his bags. Digging into his duffel, he found his phone—a palm-size unit that used an encoded satellite line. He dialed the number from memory then glanced at his watch as it rang. It was almost one-thirty in the morning, but where he was calling they didn't sleep.

The woman who answered didn't acknowledge him in any way. She simply began to speak.

"You had a call at 1:40 a.m. central standard time."

He calculated quickly. The south of Baja was an hour behind CST. The original call had come into the center more than forty-five minutes ago. He waited for the operator to continue, but she said nothing else.

"No message?"

"The subject hung up. The number was private. It originated from Austin, in Texas—"

His chest suddenly felt as if someone had put a vise around it and was squeezing hard. Gabriel interrupted the woman's mechanical voice, his own a growl. "She didn't say anything? Are you sure?"

"No verbal communication was recorded."

Gabriel digested the answer, his brain flashing through a thousand possibilities, none of them good. In the silence that followed, the woman spoke again.

"Do you have instructions?"

"If she calls back, give her this number." Gabriel read off his cell phone number. "Then you call me and let me know she phoned. Try to get her to talk to you."

"Anything else?"

Find out what's happened and why she's calling

me after all these years. Ask her if she still hates me.
Ask her if she's okay.

Ask her if she can ever forgive me.

"No," he said after a long moment. "That's all."

He punched the end key on the phone and stuffed
the tiny unit into his pocket, stunned disbelief coming
over him. Why now? What was going on with Alexis
that she was desperate enough to call him?

Totally disconcerted, Gabriel walked out to the
sandy beach. At the water's edge he stopped and
stared. The Pacific rolled in and out as steadily as it
had before, but all at once the waves looked more
hazardous, the empty blackness more menacing.

The world was suddenly a more dangerous place.

ALEX FINGERED the silken teddy, her eyes searching
the lingerie department for Libby. Ben's daughter had
pointed out the expensive pink and ivory confection
when they'd first seen it, and Alex had decided right
then it would make the perfect Christmas present for
the young woman. Looking around, Alexis spotted
Libby's tall form and red hair in the next section—
she'd already moved on to the sweaters. Quickly lo-
cating the proper size, Alex took her selection to the
counter and waited in line to pay for it, her mind
slipping away from the task at hand and back to the
subject she most wanted to forget.

A week had passed since she'd called Gabriel
O'Rourke, and every day she'd cursed herself for being so stupid. She'd hung up without saying a word,

but why on earth had she even dialed the number? It had been a ridiculous move and pointless as well. There had to be some reasonable explanation for why her drawing was missing. Her apartment had been locked and nothing else disturbed. No one could have gotten in without picking the lock, and why do that without stealing anything but a sketch? She must have put the picture somewhere and just forgotten about it. She'd been completely stressed out the past few weeks—it was entirely possible she'd done just that. Scary but possible.

The feeling had persisted—intensified even—that someone was watching her and maybe following her, as well. She'd even thought she'd seen a figure dressed in black standing beside her car the other night after she'd left the movies. She'd managed to convince herself she'd been imagining that, too, but...

Someone said something to her and Alex realized she was at the head of the line and others behind her were waiting. Paying for her purchase, she slipped the box into her larger shopping bag and stepped away, determined not to think anymore about her situation.

She found Libby at a display counter, her hand caressing a blue cashmere pullover.

"That's gorgeous," Alex said, reaching out and touching the sweater. "The color matches your eyes perfectly. Why don't you try it on?"

Libby looked up from the sweater then around at the confusion of people and decorations. Usually outgoing and happy, she shook her head dejectedly as "Jingle Bells" blared from overhead speakers. "I'm just not in the mood, Alex. Christmas is going to be so sad...I don't want any presents."

Alex smiled gently and put her hand on top of Libby's fingers. "I know, sweetheart, and I understand completely. But your dad doesn't feel that way. He wants you to have a good Christmas."

"A good Christmas isn't possible. Not with him so sick."

"I feel the same way, but your dad's feelings are the ones we need to worry about right now." She picked up the cashmere and handed it to the young woman. "Go try it on. Then come out and show me."

Libby nodded reluctantly and Alex watched as she headed for the dressing rooms, her heart breaking over everything Libby was having to go through. The girl wasn't at all prepared to lose Ben and had no idea what to do. Her mother had passed away during childbirth and Ben had pampered his only child ever since, trying to make up for the loss, his own *and* hers. Because of this overindulgence, Libby had never been responsible for anyone, including herself. She was naive and idealistic, a college student without goals. And soon she'd be all alone.

Alex turned back to the sweaters, emotion twisting in her stomach. She'd been younger than Libby when she'd run off with Esteban, but her return home had matured her quickly. Too quickly.

Libby came out of the back and saved Alex from

further thought. The sweater looked as lovely as Alex
had known it would and she bought it immediately.
Ben had handed her his credit card and told her to
get whatever caught Libby's eye. But so far, not much
had. She was too despondent.

They shopped a few more hours, then Alex drove
Libby home. She and Ben lived off Town Lake in an
expensive enclave of huge homes. Ben had been a
stockbroker until he'd been forced by his illness to
quit. He hadn't needed to work at that point but he'd
enjoyed it. When Libby invited her in, Alex didn't
have the heart to turn her down. The house felt empty
and silent with Ben so sick. She couldn't imagine how
quiet the enormous place must seem to Libby.

They went in through the back, stopping for a minute to talk to Margaret, the housekeeper. She'd been
with the family for quite some time and Alex was
grateful that at least she was there to help keep Libby
company.

Climbing the stairs to the upper floor, Alex girded
herself. Each time she saw Ben it seemed as if he'd
shrunk another inch or two, his tall and robust frame
becoming smaller and smaller. His attitude was always terrific, though, and today was no exception.

"Hey!" he said, brightening up the minute they
walked into his bedroom. "How are my two favorite
girls? Did you spend all my money? I hope you did."

Alex crossed the room and dropped a kiss on his
forehead. He winked one blue eye and gave her a
rakish grin.

"We spent as much as we could," she said. "But we might need to make a second pass to totally decimate your bank account." She sat down on the edge of his bed and took his hand in hers.

"Have at it," he said, smiling at his daughter. "That's what money's for." Patting the other side of the mattress, he directed Libby to sit down as well and tell him what they'd bought.

Alex listened to their conversation with half an ear. Ben had had his hands full when they'd married. Libby, at fourteen, had been upset and anxious about her coming teenage years. Without a mother to consult, she'd begun to get confused and make some bad choices. On one of their trips to his daughter's therapist, Ben had seen a watercolor Alex had done, which was hanging in the waiting room. Intrigued by the piece, he'd tracked her down and asked her about her work.

During the years right after Los Lobos—the empty years, she called them—Alex's art had been her saving grace but she hadn't told Ben that. Even if she had been free to explain, how do you tell someone you're not the person you were in the past? How do you tell him your name isn't your own and your life is all fiction? How can you account for your life when you're dead?

Instead, she'd talked about her painting, and by the end of the evening he'd asked her out for the following night. Successful and stable, Ben had represented everything Alex had lost. He made her feel safe again.

Two months later, when he asked her to marry him, she impulsively said yes.

But things didn't work out. Her swinging moods and black days distressed him, and after a while she felt smothered. She walked out before the inevitable happened and he left her.

Ben pulled Alex back into the conversation. "You'll be here for Christmas, right?" He squeezed her hand with the barest of motions. "Come on Christmas Eve and spend the night."

She smiled. "I'd love to do that. Nothing could keep me from Margaret's French toast."

He nodded then a darkness passed through his eyes. He was getting tired.

"I'd better go." Alex rose. "I started a new watercolor last night and I'm anxious to get back to it."

He held on to her hand then turned to Libby. "Would you give us a minute, baby? I have some Christmas secrets I need to discuss with Alex."

"Sure, Dad. No problem." She looked over at Alex. "Thanks for taking me shopping."

"We'll do it again," Alex promised. "You call me."

Ben waited until the door shut, then his gaze went back to Alex's face. "What's wrong?" he said abruptly. "You look exhausted...and worried."

He'd always been a perceptive man and his illness had not robbed that from him. "I'm fine, Ben. You don't need to be worrying about me right now."

"I'll worry more if you don't talk to me."

"It's nothing," she insisted.

He stared at her from the bed. "I don't have time for lies, Alex. Tell me what's bothering you."

His bluntness did just what he'd planned on it doing. Alex sat back down. "You know me too well."

"No," he replied with a small smile. "I *don't* know you, even after all this time. And that was part of the problem, wasn't it?" He waited, but when she didn't answer, he spoke again. "Talk to me."

Uncertain of how to explain, she looked down at her hands and gathered her thoughts. There was no way to make it all sound reasonable, so she just started. "I've had that creepy feeling again. The one where I feel like someone is…" She hesitated. "…is watching me. And the other night, when I came home, I was sure someone was in my apartment."

"Did you call the police?"

"No." As she answered, she thought of the call she *had* made then she pushed the memory aside. "I didn't want to look like the fool I did last time this happened."

"I take it no one was there?"

She shook her head. "The place was empty."

"But…"

She raised her eyes to his. She obviously couldn't tell him about the sketch, because he knew nothing of her family.

"But nothing," she said, shrugging. "It just bothered me that I thought someone had been there. I don't want to go nuts again."

He laughed despite the seriousness of their conversation. "You didn't 'go nuts.' You had a bad patch, that's all. Lots of people go through problems like that."

Their eyes connected over the bedsheets. "Lots of people have problems, Ben, but they don't try to kill themselves."

"You didn't mean it."

"Oh, yes, I did." She fingered one of the wide gold bracelets she always wore on her wrists. He'd commented on the pieces their wedding night and she'd been forced to explain the two-inch vertical scars they hid—the dividing lines, she called them, the before-and-after lines. "Believe me, I couldn't have been *more* serious."

He waited for a second, then spoke in a quiet voice. "Do you want to move back in here? It'd be great to have you—"

"I can't do that."

"Why not?"

"Because it isn't necessary. And besides that, I wouldn't want to impose."

"Libby and I love you—it wouldn't be an imposition to have you here again. It'd be wonderful and you'd be safe and secure…" His blue eyes held all the wistfulness of a kid looking through the window at a toy store. He wanted their past back, she realized all at once, desperately wanted to replay their time together, when he had protected her from anything and everything, including herself.

The horrible irony hit her hard. What would Ben do—right here and now—to have the opportunity she'd had to start over with life? To begin again with everything different? She hadn't been dying, of course, but she'd done everything she could to make that happen.

If she'd stopped to think about, she would have realized she'd been considering her options ever since her drawing had been taken, but she'd needed Ben— needed this moment—to come to a turning point. She stood up, determination in her voice.

"I'm thirty years old, Ben. It's time I look my demons in the eye and deal with them, one way or the other. And no one can do that for me. I have to do it myself." She leaned over and kissed him on the forehead. "I should have dealt with this a long time ago, but I was too scared. I really appreciate your offer, though."

"What changed your mind?"

"Nothing. I still feel the same. I'm terrified..." She gripped his hand and blinked. "But I can't hide any longer. Now I'm too scared *not* to look..."

ALEX MADE HER WAY HOME through rush-hour traffic. It wasn't as bad as usual, but was still heavy and by the time she reached her side of town she was too tired to even heat a frozen dinner. She decided to treat herself to dinner at her favorite restaurant, Fonda San Miguel.

She didn't know what she was going to do, but

simply making the decision to do *something* about her past seemed to free her. Feeling herself relax for the first time in weeks, she had a wonderful meal, including dessert. She was shocked to see an hour and a half had passed when her waiter finally presented the check. After a final cup of coffee, she paid the tab and left.

The restaurant was tucked away in a residential area, and huge trees bordered the building and parking lot. Alex tried to hang on to the mellow feeling she'd developed inside, but the minute she walked out the heavy carved door, something didn't feel right. The parking lot felt empty and dark. She almost turned around and went back inside, but then what would she do? Ask someone to walk back out to her car with her? Call the police and tell them how crazy she was feeling?

Neither option seemed viable, so instead she kept going.

By the time she reached her car, her heart was careening out of control, her breath coming too fast, her pulse racing. With a trembling hand, she hastily unlocked the vehicle and climbed inside, throwing the locks behind her before she did anything else.

She sat for a moment and tried to calm herself but she had no luck. Shadows loomed against the other cars and she heard sounds she couldn't decipher. When a car backfired several streets over, she jumped. Oddly enough, the reflexive action seemed to break her trance. She chastised herself for the paranoia and laughing shakily, she put the car in gear and drove home.

Back at her apartment complex, Alex loaded her arms with the packages from her shopping trip and started up the sidewalk. Christmas music wafted out from beneath someone's door along with the sound of laughter. She felt better than she had back at the restaurant, but she didn't dawdle, crossing the poolside area and quickly making her way up the stairs. She stepped inside, juggling the shopping bags and boxes, but her blinds were closed.

Puzzled, she put everything down on the entry table then felt her way to the light switch, stopping first at the window. Twirling the rod that hung to one side, she flipped the slats upward and light immediately flooded the living room.

There was a man sitting in the chair.

But this time he wasn't a stranger. This time she knew who he was.

CHAPTER FIVE

GABRIEL MET ALEXIS MISSION'S startled stare with a steady one of his own. The past swirled between them, the tension between them a physical presence.

He'd been watching her for almost a week. On the surface, everything seemed fine, but her nervous anxiety had been obvious. She was barely balanced on a high beam of confusion and fright—anything might send her over. He wanted to walk away and leave her to it.

But he couldn't.

Still staring at him, she didn't say a word. Instead, she came to where he sat and stood above him. She looked as if she was reconciling something in her mind. For a moment he was confused, then suddenly he understood. He'd seen *her* countless times in the last ten years but all she had of him was a single memory, a night she couldn't forget.

But she knew who he was.

"What are you doing here?"

Her voice had changed just like the rest of her.

Deeper and more resonant, it was husky and hinted at the tough times she'd gone through and survived.

"You called me."

She hesitated, taking her time to carefully form the answer. "That phone call was a mistake."

"A mistake?" He raised one eyebrow.

They waited in the ticking silence and stared at each other. Downstairs a party started to break up. Gabriel could hear a door slam and people spilling on to the sidewalk, their laughter accompanied by Christmas music and shouts of good cheer. The jarring sounds were so at odds with what was happening between them, they seemed to come from another time, another world—a place where people celebrated holidays and enjoyed their moments together.

When the stillness returned, he spoke softly. "You don't just dial a memorized number after ten years *by mistake.*"

She moved toward the window, splitting the blinds with two fingers to look down. Standing there in silence, her form so slight, her face distressed, she didn't seem real to Gabriel. The whole situation had the feeling of a dream.

She stared out at the night for what felt like a long time, then she turned. With the outside lights streaming in from behind her, he couldn't see her face.

"I got scared and I called you. But I shouldn't have. It was nothing."

"Why don't you tell me what 'it' was and let me decide what's nothing."

She bristled. "I don't need you or your help. I've managed the past ten years on my own, just fine, no thanks to you."

"'Just fine...'?" He shook his head, his gaze going to the wide bracelets she wore on her wrists. "Are you sure about that? I don't think I'd describe your success that way."

Her eyes flared. "You've kept tabs on me?"

He held his hands out, palms up, then dropped them.

"For how long?"

He didn't answer, but he didn't have to. She knew.

Like a spark buffeted by wind, her anger flickered then went out. She sat down on the sofa, her nails— short and unpolished—glittering in the light coming through the front window. Gabriel waited in silence as she gripped the arms of the couch and tried to absorb the reality of his presence and what that meant. After a few moments, she spoke, her voice strangely flat.

"Sometimes I think I see them."

He needed a second to understand, then when he did, he wished he hadn't. "That's not possible."

"I know that...but it happens before I can remember." She paused. "Lately it's happened a lot."

Gabriel closed his eyes for a heartbeat. He saw them, too, but now it was only in his dreams. Because

six months after he'd told Alexis her parents were
dead, the lie had been partially fulfilled. Gabriel *had
seen* Robert Mission all right; he'd been lying in a
casket.

René Cuvier, Guy's brother, had shot him.

The government, no matter how much the Missions
had done, hadn't been able to keep them safe. With
Robert's murder, Selena disappeared, the baby already hidden safely with a family who loved him,
legally adopted by them, new name included. Gabriel
had no idea where Selena had gone, and frankly he
didn't *want* to know. It was safer for her—and for
him—that way.

In the dim light, Alex's features remained still,
carved out of marble, white and expressionless. The
only motion he could detect came from deep within
her eyes, a quick flash of gold and green that disappeared as soon as he saw it.

He leaned forward in his chair. "Tell me why you
called, Alexis."

"Don't call me that," she said sharply. "I go by
Alex now."

"All right." He spoke calmly, carefully, as if to a
child. "Tell me why you called, Alex. It might be
important."

"It wasn't," she insisted.

"You don't know that." He paused and thought of
what a bastard he was. "If something has happened
to you, I need to know. It could be dangerous…"

Her expression did change, then. A look of alarm came swiftly, her eyes growing wide. In a familiar gesture, her hand went to her neck. She had on the same piece of jewelry she'd worn that night. A small, gold heart on a chain so thin it almost seemed invisible.

"Tell me," he said. "Tell me why you called."

She held out for a few more minutes and he remembered that night, how she'd try to flee him. How later he'd watched her sleep. How the sky had turned purple when her plane flew off.

She'd led a very troubled life and she had no one to blame but him. *He* was the one who'd recruited Robert and Selena. *He* was the one who'd set up the operation from the very beginning, pulling the two innocent scientists into his world of violence to help him catch Guy Cuvier. They had been patriots. He was nothing but a hired gun.

Gabriel picked up the familiar burden of guilt he'd been carrying for ten years. "Alexis?" he said deliberately.

She turned then and looked him in the eye.

"Tell me." He spoke as if asking an old friend how they'd been doing—in a soft, almost conversational voice. Underneath the silk, though, there was steel. "Tell me what's happened...."

ALEX HAD SEEN his gaze a thousand times in her dreams, but she'd forgotten the darkness that lived behind it. There were other things she'd forgotten, too, or maybe, in the intervening years, they'd changed. The way his hair curled, the slant of his mouth, the angles of his face. Each of his features was as cold and cruel-looking as before, but something about him, about the *totality* of him, was different.

She wouldn't have thought it possible, but it seemed as if the years had honed him, had whetted the edges that had been there before, throwing them into even deeper relief.

The blackness that surrounded him came from a place deep inside his soul, a buried emotion that bubbled and burned. If it ever escaped, surely disaster would follow.

She realized what she was doing and gave herself a mental shake. Why did she even care what kind of man he was? All she needed from him was information. She cursed herself again for making the stupid mistake of calling him.

"There's really nothing to tell," she said with a shrug. "I panicked the other night when I came home after swimming and I called you. I thought someone had been inside my apartment. But that was you, wasn't it? I don't like—"

"No." He interrupted her, his dark eyes drilling hers. "It wasn't me. I've never been in here before."

Something in his voice, in his manner, came across the space between them and she found herself believing him, just as she had that night ten years ago when he'd told her she'd be safe. This illogical reaction to his words made her angry, although she couldn't explain why.

"Don't lie to me." She tightened her mouth, felt her lips go into a line of bitterness. "Not now. Not after everything you've put me through."

"I was the cleanup man, Alex. Nothing more. Nothing less."

"Now I know you're lying," she retorted. "I've never believed that."

"I'm well aware of that fact," he said. "You made your feelings on the subject more than clear the last time we were together."

"Well, they haven't changed. You know more about this situation than you're letting on. You always have."

His gaze hardened imperceptibly. "And what makes you think that?"

"The government wouldn't send someone like you to simply clean up the situation. That doesn't make sense. It wouldn't be logical."

He made a sound of derision and shook his head. "You're giving Uncle Sam more credit than he deserves. Logic isn't something he's familiar with."

"Is that a trait you share with him?"

They stared at each other, stripes of light painting their faces.

"What did they take?" he asked abruptly.

She jerked in surprise, then tried to hide the reaction by standing. "What are you talking about?"

He answered patiently, willing—for a while—to play her game. "The person who came into your apartment—what did he take?"

"You can answer that question better than I can."

"If I had been in your apartment, we wouldn't be having this conversation." His pause was deliberate and long. "You would not have known anyone had been here."

His words hung in the air, their inherent threat so subtle she felt it slide over her skin, a physical sensation.

"But I'm willing to bet money I know what's gone." He waited a beat then spoke again. "It's something you shouldn't have had...something that meant more to you than anything. Something to do with your family."

Shocked into silence, Alex took a step backward, her profile blocking the light and sending his face into darkness. Denial was the only way she could fight back. She tried, but the words sounded lame, even to her. "There's no way you could possibly know that unless you're the one who took it."

"That's not true." His voice was so soft she had to strain to hear him.

"Then how—"

"I know *you*. It's the only reason you would have called."

SHE MOVED AWAY from the window and came back to sit on the sofa. As she passed him, he caught a whiff of her perfume. The scent was different from what she'd worn before, something spicy and complex. The other one had been a simple floral, maybe lilac? He couldn't remember despite the fact it had stayed with him long past the time it should have.

He only knew one thing for certain. Nothing about Alexis—Alex—was the same.

He'd seen hints of this from afar, but up close, talking to her, sitting with her in the same room, the changes struck him even harder. She was wary and nervous, a constant state of tension etching its way across her features. Her eyes weren't blank anymore, but what they held now was almost worse. She'd seen the bad side of life and it had left more than sadness. Their hazel depths were full of something Gabriel didn't want to even name.

The only familiar thing about her was the color of her hair. She'd kept it blond, although a softer, more flattering shade than he'd picked out that night at the drugstore. Briefly he wondered why, then she spoke again and distracted him from the thought.

"You don't know who I am," she said harshly. "You don't have the slightest idea."

"Then why don't you tell me who you are."

"I'm not telling you anything."

She crossed her arms and looked at him with the same kind of defiance he'd seen ten years earlier.

Underneath the attitude, though, Gabriel saw a layer of fear.

"What did they take?" he asked again.

She looked away from him, then her gaze came back. Reluctantly. "I sketched the photograph you took from me that night. I...I kept it beside my bed in a silver frame. It's gone."

Keeping his expression blank, Gabriel absorbed the news. This wasn't a good development. Not good at all.

He started to say so, then he stopped himself. There was more to the situation than Alexis had shared with him. There had to be. She was keeping something back, something he wouldn't like, he decided rapidly.

He could play it low-key or confront her. Which would work best? It didn't take long for him to decide. Alex was already off-kilter—he'd be stupid not to take advantage of that fact.

The living room was small, so small that his knees were almost touching hers. Without any warning, he reached out and grabbed her wrist, locking his fingers tightly around it. "What are hiding from me?"

Caught off guard exactly as Gabriel had hoped, Alex flinched. Her reaction generated a fleeting moment of admiration from him as she tried to wrench her hand out of his grip. He held on long enough to scare her a bit more, then he opened his hand and released her.

"I have nothing to hide from you." Rubbing her

wrist, she stared defiantly at him. He could see her pulse jumping at the base of her neck. "You're the one with all the secrets. If anyone here needs to confess, I think it's you."

He hid his reaction as she spoke again.

"In fact," she said, "if anything, I think I've *underestimated* you all these years."

"You don't know what you're talking about."

She stared at him with distrust, then she seemed to give up on him, frustration filling her hazel eyes. She spoke abruptly. "Do you want something to drink?"

The timing couldn't have been better. He'd gotten what he could from her, at least for tonight. Anything more and she'd close up completely.

He knew she didn't drink alcohol anymore, but he wondered if she kept it in the house.

"Scotch?" he asked.

She gave him the answer he'd expected. "I usually keep some for guests. I'll check."

He nodded. Just as he'd thought—that particular temptation no longer held sway over Alex Worthington. She was a strong woman.

She walked into the kitchen and a few moments later he heard a cabinet opening. A second after that came the sound of the refrigerator door and then the clink of ice.

Moving soundlessly, Gabriel made his way to the front door, slipped it open and stepped outside, closing it softly behind him. The night embraced him and then he was gone.

ALEX PICKED UP her ginger ale and Gabriel's drink then left the kitchen, speaking as she came out. "The scotch was all gone so I fixed you something…"

Her voice trailed off when she saw the empty living room. Frowning, she set the glasses on the coffee table, her eyes going down the hall toward the other rooms. Was he checking out her bedroom?

She moved quickly to the back of the apartment, looking into each doorway as she passed it. By the time she'd reached the bathroom, she knew he had left, disappearing without a word while she'd been in the kitchen.

Walking back to the living room, Alex was shaken. Why had he taken off so suddenly? Where had he gone? As dangerous as that process could be, any scrap of information she might be able to mine from him would help her put the past all together.

She picked up her tumbler and moved to the window, sipping as she peered thoughtfully out the blinds. When she'd walked in, she'd been terrified to see him. As their conversation had progressed and she'd begun to realize he wasn't going to help, all she'd wanted was to get him out as fast as possible. Now he was gone, and she found herself wishing he hadn't left.

Her reaction didn't make any sense—but nothing about this situation did.

It never had.

ALEX SPENT the rest of the night trying to put Gabriel O'Rourke's visit behind her. Conflicting arguments ran through her head; she needed him, but didn't want him to know what she was doing.

Despite the tension, his dark eyes and even darker nature kept intruding. By sunrise Friday morning, she impulsively decided the only thing that might help her was a trip to Los Lobos, where everything had started. Gabriel had told her never to do that, of course, but after all this time, it couldn't matter. If she wanted answers—and not from Gabriel—she had to go back to where this disaster had begun.

She didn't want to give herself enough time to think about it. Calling the airline, she reserved a seat, dressed and headed straight for the airport. The flight from Austin to Dallas was a short one, the route on to Albuquerque almost as quick. She was on the road to Los Lobos faster than she could have imagined.

The air was cold and dry, drifts from a recent snow still marking the streets and sidewalks. She couldn't help but compare the trip—and her emotions—to the time she'd been there before.

She slowed as she entered the town limits, but almost on its own, it seemed, the car found the street and then the house where her parents and baby

brother had lived so long ago. The residence where
the older couple had lived was empty and for sale.
The door opened to the home on the other side—
where the younger woman and babies had lived—and
a black man came out. Without looking her way, he
climbed into an SUV, backed out the driveway and
left.

Her attention returned to the house in the middle.
She didn't mean to stop, but she parked by the curb
to stare. The outside woodwork had been repainted,
the glistening facade revealing new owners and new
dreams. A well-tended yard held Christmas decorations—a Santa and Rudolph, his red nose blinking, a
dusting of snow over both of them. As Alex sat there,
the front door suddenly gaped wide and three young
children tumbled out. They were dressed warmly and
immediately began to gather up the small piles of
snow that dotted the yard. A second later, a woman
came out of the house as well. Her hands on the porch
railing, she laughed at the children's antics until she
glanced up and saw Alex's car. Her expression turned
curious and then a little concerned. There was nothing
Alex could do but put the car in gear and drive away.

She turned blindly at the corner, an unexpected on-
slaught of emotions hitting her hard. A part of her
had hoped she might be able to go inside, but for what
reason she didn't know. All of her parents' things
were long gone, any evidence of their life there totally
erased.

Just like them. Just like her.

Alex headed downtown, then took the cut off toward the interstate. The Mansfield Operations Center came up unexpectedly, the empty land between the think tank and town now filled with warehouses and other commercial buildings. She slowed as she neared the entrance, then pulled off the road when she drew close. The gate was padlocked, the guard shack in shambles. The whole operation had obviously been shut down for quite some time, she saw with dismay. What had happened to all the scientists who had worked there with her parents? She had no idea what they'd even done, she realized with a start. Her mother had explained it once, but the childhood definition was woefully inadequate now.

We're making the world safer, honey. It's a wonderful place to work.

With a sigh of disappointment, Alex turned the car around and drove back to town. Coming to Los Lobos had been a big mistake. What on earth had she thought she would accomplish? Exiting the freeway, she returned to the center of town. She'd had nothing to eat all day. She'd stop and grab something, then she'd return to Albuquerque and catch the next flight to Austin. There was nothing for her here, no information, no recollections.

Halfway down the second block, Alex stopped at a red light. Looking to her left, she realized suddenly that she was in front of the gas station where she'd asked directions that night. The pumps had been re-moved and a parking lot installed. The building itself had been converted into a diner.

The light changed and someone behind Alex honked. The sound jarred her into action and she swung into the lot at the very last minute. She had to eat anyway; this place was probably as good as the next.

The inside of the former gasoline station looked nothing like it had before. Everything had been ripped out, of course, and now a long bar with stools stretched across the length of the building, booths with red plastic seats lining the windows. Only the memorabilia on the walls gave a hint of what had been there before. An old Esso sign dotted the area behind the grill and a red Pegasus hung to its right.

The place was fairly busy considering the late hour, the waitresses still harried. Alex took one of the stools at the bar and ordered a salad. By the time her meal came and she ate it, things had begun to settle down a bit.

She dabbed her lips and watched the hostess. The woman had to be in her seventies, maybe even older, her ankles swollen, her gray hair pulled back. Despite her age, she hadn't stopped once since Alex had come in. Cheerful and gregarious, she seemed to know everyone perched at the counter and half of those in the booths. She'd chatted with each person in turn, filling their mugs with coffee and their ears with gossip.

After a bit, she made her way to Alex's spot, a steaming glass pot in her hand. "More coffee, miss?"

"That'd be great." Alex pushed the mug closer and smiled. "This is certainly a busy place. Have you been open long?"

The waitress filled Alex's mug and gave her a friendly look. "Not from around here, huh?"

"No, I'm not." Alex added sugar to her coffee. "But my parents lived here for a little while. About ten years ago."

The waitress lifted her eyebrows. "Ten years ago? That's just about the time we opened." She shook her head. "Business wasn't always this good, that's for sure. People didn't want to come in at first, much less eat. Took some time for everybody to forget."

Something tingled along the back of Alex's neck. "To forget what?" she asked carefully.

"The murder."

Alex took a sip of her coffee then put the mug back down. "There was a murder here?" She pointed at the floor and tried to keep her hand from shaking. *"Right here?"*

"You betcha." The older woman leaned closer to the bar. "An old guy owned the place. Sold gas. Somebody came in here and killed him. Strangled him with one of those thingies made outta wire. Almost cut his head off. There was blood everywhere the way I heard it. A terrible mess. An awful trag-edy.''

Alex felt the color leave her face. She hoped the woman didn't notice. "Th-that's awful," she man-aged to say. "Did they find the killer?"

"Oh, no… Whoever did it got clean away. The mystery's never been solved and that's a real shame, too. His widow has passed, but I'm sure she had to think about it every year 'bout this time.''

Alex lifted her eyes, her heart thumping so hard she could barely hear herself speak. She tried her best to keep her voice steady. "Why is that?"

The waitress picked up her coffeepot. "Well, she's the one who found him. Brought him a plate with turkey and dressing. The cops said she dropped the plate and food went everywhere. Messed up their in-vestigating.'' She shook her head soulfully. "Helluva thing to happen on Thanksgiving night."

CHAPTER SIX

THE RETURN TRIP to Texas passed in a haze of disbelief. When Alex unlocked the door to her apartment and stepped inside, she felt as though she'd been in New Mexico one minute, and a second later back in Austin. She didn't remember anything of the drive from Los Lobos to the airport or of the flights themselves. The whole journey was a blank.

Dropping her purse to the floor, she immediately looked to her right. The living room was empty, thank God, and the rest of the apartment proved to be the same. After checking every room twice, she came slowly down the hall and collapsed on the sofa, closing her eyes and rubbing them in a gesture of weariness.

The old man had been murdered. With a garrote. Sometime after he'd given Alex directions to Mansfield.

The images that came with that thought were too much to bear. Ignoring her exhaustion, Alex jumped up from the sofa as if moving would scare them away. She went into the kitchen and poured herself a large

glass of milk, then walked determinedly back into her
bedroom where she busied herself with drawing a
bath and preparing for bed.

An hour later, with the lights off and the apartment
quiet, Alex was slipping into an uneasy sleep when
she remembered something. The words hit her with a
jolt, almost as if they'd been spoken out loud. She sat
up, recalling Gabriel's ominous answer that night to
her question about the guard at Mansfield.

"He's been taken care of."

All at once, her mouth went dry. What did "taken
care of" mean exactly? She struggled to remember
the rest of the conversation. Snatches came back to
her haltingly.

"No one must know anything about you..."

"You can not go back to Los Lobos. Ever."

*"If you hadn't shown up, this might not have been
a problem, but you did, so now we have to deal with
it. That's why I'm here."*

Had she told Gabriel she'd gotten directions from
the old man? She couldn't remember, but if he'd been
following her, Gabriel would have had plenty of time
to kill the gas station attendant and then go back and
wait for her.

Had Gabriel O'Rourke murdered a defenseless old
man ten years ago?

Her heart thumping wildly, Alex stared into the
darkness and contemplated the possibilities. She
didn't go to sleep until the sun came up, her last con-

scious thought an uneasy acknowledgment that there
was only one person on earth who could answer that
question.

THE PREVIOUS WEEK Gabriel had found South Lamar,
where a half-dozen sleazy used-car lots lined the bou-
levard. He'd looked around and selected the seediest,
which was saying quite a bit. Under a faded sign in
the shape of a cactus, the haphazardly parked vehicles
were just what he'd expected—student castoffs that
barely ran, with worn tires and scraped paint.

They were perfect.

The salesman didn't blink an eye when Gabriel selected the cheapest thing on the lot. He did blink at
the cash. When Gabriel added an extra fifty "for the
good service," the man's face cleared and he handed
the keys over without a word. Five minutes later, Gabriel was driving away in a Toyota no one would ever
remember.

He'd been parked on Alex's street, more or less,
ever since. He blended in completely. Looked, in fact,
like every other aging hippie in the college-dominated
town, a little down on his luck but not really caring.
No one, including Alex, had noticed him, and after
several days of too much caffeine and too many cigarettes, he'd seen exactly what he thought he would.

Returning to his spot on Sunday afternoon, Gabriel
cut off the car's engine and parked. He'd trailed Alex
to the airport on Friday and realized she'd gone back

to Los Lobos. For two seconds, he'd thought of going with her, but he'd turned away when she'd gotten on the plane. There was no danger for her in New Mexico.

It'd left there and come to Texas.

He stared across the street at her building. She might have seen the complex as secure—it had gates and a rent-a-cop who patrolled when the urge struck him—but anyone could get inside. While Alexis had been gone, he had...and very easily at that. Just as easily, he imagined, as whoever had been in her apartment and stolen her drawing.

He'd pondered the possibilities of who that could be from the moment he'd left her, but nothing he came up with made any sense. Even more heavy on his mind, however, had been Alexis's attitude. She'd been frightened and rightly so. But why now? After all these years? The question plagued him but he was patient. In time, he'd know. Either Alexis would tell him or he'd force her hand.

Warming his palms on a cup of convenience-store coffee, Gabriel corrected himself. She was "Alex" now, not Alexis. The Agency had changed her name along with the rest of her existence. That fact had struck him hard when he'd searched her apartment. Cold and stark, the only touch of life in her place had come from one of her unfinished paintings.

He'd stared at the glowing canvas for a long time, marveling at her talent. He'd seen her work before, but viewing it this way—uncompleted—he was struck fresh by her creativity. The exotic colors and swirling depths hinted at such passion, they had transfixed him.

Afterward, he decided he shouldn't have been surprised. During the rough years, her art had been the only thing anchoring her to any kind of reality. She'd done her damnedest to self-destruct and she'd almost succeeded before meeting Ben Worthington. Gabriel blew on his coffee, his grudging acceptance of what the man had done for Alex a burdensome admittance. When he'd learned of the older man's bad health, Gabriel had wondered what impact Worthington's imminent death would have on Alex. Would she handle his "abandonment" as she'd handled her parents?

Alex's front door opened unexpectedly and she stepped into the clear and cold Texas afternoon. She carried a large leather portfolio in one hand, a tackle box in the other. She hesitated long enough on the outside landing to make Gabriel wonder if she would leave or not. Finally, she made her way down the stairs and to her car. He reached for the keys of the wreck. The engine complained but turned over and he pulled out into the traffic to follow her.

ALEX EASED onto the MoPac Highway and headed north. The exit to Zilker came up quickly, and she found a parking space near Barton Springs Road. Normally crowded with tourists and college kids in the summer, the park and botanical gardens were almost deserted this time of year. She took a deep breath and headed for the Moon Bridge. The tranquil spot never failed to bring her peace, and after her trip, peace was definitely what she needed.

For half a second, after stepping outside back at the apartment, she'd wondered how smart it was to go somewhere like the park. Out on the landing, she could have sworn she felt eyes on her. The desire to retreat had been so strong it reminded her of her past, of how she'd escaped her pain before using all the wrong techniques. That thought was all it took; she'd resolutely slammed the door behind her and left.

Now, heading down the trail, she was glad she'd come. The air felt so clean it seemed to wash her, the sky above that particular shade of blue that existed nowhere else but Texas. Within a few minutes, she found the little bridge with its water lilies and rocky ledge. The greenery that usually surrounded the secluded scene had fallen victim to the latest freeze, but there was still a beauty to the place. In a matter of minutes, she had everything set up and, using the Impressionist style that was her trademark, she set to work. Galleries all over town requested her watercolors but this one would be just for her. For her peace of mind.

Two hours later, Alex stepped back from her canvas and considered the results with a tilt of her head. She stood for several minutes, but before she could decide if she liked the painting or not, the noise of a sliding footfall came down the path toward her. The sound was almost—but not quite—silent, and that scared her more than anything. The isolation that had seemed so serene before suddenly turned into a liability. She froze.

And Gabriel came around the corner.

As usual, he wore black and a cold expression, his eyes two dark stones of secrecy. Alex swallowed and tried to act as if she weren't frightened, but all she could do was remember the old lady's words. *"There was blood everywhere…almost cut his head off… never been solved…"*

Lifting the brush she still held, Alex wiped it carefully on one of her rags then she forced her gaze to meet his. "Do you ever ask anyone to meet you or do you always just appear?"

He had his hands in his pockets and they stayed there as he answered. "I prefer not to be predictable."

"Why is that?"

"Once they know I'm coming, people don't usually stick around."

"I can understand that."

"I'm sure you do."

She put down her brush and hid her agitation. His ability to come from nowhere kept her off balance, which was, of course, the point of it, she was sure. Reaching over, she closed the lid to a plastic jar of water sitting on a nearby rock then she straightened.

"What are you doing here? Somehow I doubt you came to see the sights."

"I want to hear about Los Lobos. How was it?"

She wasn't surprised that he knew. "The trip went fine," she said in a noncommittal voice.

"What did you learn?"

"What makes you think I went there to learn anything?"

"You went there for a reason." He shrugged. "I thought you might want to share it with me. I could help—"

She spoke sharply, despite her earlier thoughts. "I told you I don't want your help. You've done enough already—"

"This isn't a conversation to be having in a public place." He took a step in her direction. "Besides that, it's getting cold...and late."

She considered his words and realized he had a point. After a moment, she tilted her head to indicate the street that ran past the park. "There's a bar just down this road. Not on the main drag—two lights over, behind all the restaurants. It's a Mexican place called Hector's. We can talk there."

"A bar isn't more private—"

"Believe me, no one will bother us." She paused, her past catching up with her for the second time that day. "I used to go there for that very reason. It's a hole in the wall. We'll be alone."

SHE HADN'T LIED. Hector's was a real dump. Dark and grungy, the place reeked of dead cigarettes and old disappointments. There was no comparison to be made—either between the establishments or the women—but for some reason the whole setup reminded Gabriel of the last time he'd been in a dimly lit bar with a drink in his hand and a woman by his side. Following Alex deeper into the gloom, Gabriel shoved the memory to the spot in his brain where he kept past disasters. There were plenty of other catastrophes there—it wouldn't be alone.

She went straight to a booth in the back, her steps so determined he could tell it had been "hers" when she'd been a regular.

A burly Hispanic came from behind the bar to their table. In Spanish, Alex ordered a beer for Gabriel and a ginger ale for herself. They said nothing to each other until the man brought the bottles, put them down and faded once more to the back.

Gabriel drank half the beer before setting it down. "Tell me about Los Lobos."

Even in the darkness, he could see her tense.

"I don't want you following me. I'm perfectly all right and I don't—"

"—need my help," he supplied. "I know that's what you think but you're thinking wrong." He took another mouthful of beer, watching her above the tilted bottle.

"And why am I wrong?" She mimicked his movement and drank.

"Because I'm not the only one who's been following you."

Swallowing audibly, she set her bottle down with a thud. "Someone else is following me?"

He nodded.

Her face took on a stunned expression, his pronouncement either totally unexpected or confirmation of a long-held fear. She spoke and he knew it was the latter.

"Good God, all this time I thought I might be imagining it…" She blinked. "Then I thought it was you… Now this…"

"I *was* watching you," he confirmed. "But there's somebody else out there, too. I spotted the car once last week and again yesterday. It's a dirty, white Lexus, older model, tinted windows. Any idea who that might be?"

She frowned, a slight furrow plowing its way across her brow. "I can't think of anyone… Was it a man or a woman?"

He shrugged. "Couldn't tell. The plates came back stolen. I tailed them but they lost me. I don't know if it was on purpose or just luck."

She looked over his shoulder, into the dim corners of the tiny bar. "Who do you think it is?" she asked after a while, her eyes coming back to his.

"I don't know. I was hoping you could answer that question."

"Do you think…" She stopped and unconsciously pulled at her bottom lip with her upper teeth. "Do you think whoever it is was associated with…you know."

"Your parents?"

She nodded reluctantly.

"I have no idea. But I've made some calls. I've got a buddy who still works at the Agency. We're meeting soon. He might be able to tell me something."

Gabriel let her absorb this news, then he leaned closer. He caught the faint scent of paint and fresh air as she looked up at him, her eyes dark with the reflections of too many ghosts.

"I've shown you mine," he said. "Now you show me yours."

"Wh—what do you mean?"

He held his hands out above the table. "I gave you some information. I want some in return."

"Like what?"

"For starters, what you did in Los Lobos. You shouldn't have gone back there."

Her expression turned wary before she closed it and leaned back against the booth. Not to relax, he noted, but to get farther away from him.

"I just wanted to see the place," she said. "I

haven't been back since…since I left and I thought it was time.''

"Bullshit."

She stared at him.

He leaned even closer. "Tell me what you did."

"Or what?"

"Or you just might die."

Her composure slipped and he saw a flash of unbridled fear. But her voice didn't betray it.

"Is that a threat?" she asked.

"No. It's a real possibility. If the people who were involved in your parents' situation have found out about you, they *will* kill you. Without any thought. Killing you would be like killing a fly."

Her throat moved and he found himself watching the smooth column before she spoke and pulled his gaze back to her face.

"After all this time?"

"Time means even less to them than your life."

Despite everything, Alex let Gabriel's words wash over her. He had a voice like soft rain. In any other circumstances she would have been lulled by it, calmed by it. But not here. And not by him. At the same time, there was only one way she could get ahead. She had to give him the truth and see what he did with it.

"I went back to the house," she said. "There was a woman living there, a woman with children. They were building a snowman." She picked up her soft drink, drank some, then put it back down. "The neighbors on one side were different and the house on the other side was for sale. Everything had changed."

Gabriel nodded. "The older couple decided to live out West, closer to their children. They bought a nice big place out there."

"And the woman with the toddlers?"

"She came into some unexpected money from an aunt who passed away. I'm not sure where she is now."

Shocked that he would even tell her this much, it was Alex's turn to nod. "After that I went out to the center but it'd been closed."

"Then what?"

She took a steady breath, her hands cold and nervous. "I stopped and ate at a little diner in the middle of town. The place used to be a service station, but the owner had been killed." She lifted her gaze. "With a garrote. On Thanksgiving, ten years ago."

He looked back with unblinking eyes.

Alex gripped her ginger ale. She wanted to throw it at his head, to reach across the table and shake him, to do anything to get some kind of reaction, but she was an amateur and she knew it. Gabriel wasn't going to tell her anything he didn't want her to know. She had nothing else to lose, so she leaned closer to him. "Did you kill him?"

"No."

She didn't want to but she believed him...until something glittered in his gaze, something that made her pulse accelerate.

"But you knew he'd been killed," she guessed suddenly.

"Yes."

"Do you know who did it?"

"Yes."

They sat in silence, staring at each other, then to Alex's surprise, Gabriel blinked first. He sighed and signaled the bartender for another beer. When he had come and gone, leaving another bottle, Gabriel spoke quietly.

"Someone who was...involved in your parents' situation killed the owner of the service station. He tortured him then murdered him."

"Why?" Alex's mouth went dry. "Why would he kill a defenseless old man?"

His hesitation was so small Alex almost missed it. Almost. "I'm not really sure but I always suspected the murder had something to do with you. I couldn't find a connection between you and the old guy, though."

Her pulse buzzed like a horde of trapped bees, then the blood drained from her body. She could feel it go in a rush, leaving her light-headed and hot. She'd been responsible for the attendant's death—*she*—not Gabriel. "I—I found a matchbook in my dad's desk—it had the name of the service station and some notes on it. I went there to—to get directions to the center. I told him I was looking for my parents..."

"You told him who they were?"

"I gave him their names."

"A matchbook..." Gabriel nodded, a rueful shake of his head. "So the old guy *did* know you—I guess I wasn't too far off the mark."

With a measureless effort, Alex fought down her guilt, another even more overwhelming consideration replacing it as she realized the importance of what this all meant.

"Then the people who killed my parents...they must know—" She stopped, then started again. "They must know who I am, right? They know I exist? And they have, all this time?"

Gabriel took a drink then shook his head. "They know nothing."

"How do you know that? How can you be sure?" She glanced frantically around the bar then back at Gabriel. "For all you know, whoever's following me right now could be—"

Gabriel's hand shot across the table and he seized her arm. As it had once before, the shock of his touch was enough to silence her.

"They don't know anything about you. At least, not who you are now." His voice was harsh, his eyes hard.

"How do you know that?"

"If they did, we wouldn't be having this conversation. You'd already be dead."

HE FOLLOWED HER HOME, but this time she knew it. Alex parked in her usual spot then waited for Gabriel to pull up beside her. She hadn't wanted him to come with her—"it's not necessary," she'd halfheartedly argued—but he'd ignored her and started his car, letting her pull out of the bar's lot first.

He walked her across the patio and up the stairs, his fingertips on her elbow. The gesture was an old-fashioned one and felt strange. It was not what she would have expected from this man, but she was beginning to realize she couldn't rule out anything with Gabriel. He was an enigma she was almost afraid to solve.

They stopped outside her door and she unlocked it, the laughable idea running through her brain that anyone seeing them might think they'd just come in from a date. An unsuccessful one.

Without a word, he stepped past her and went into her apartment. She waited on the landing, and two seconds later he was back. "Everything's fine."

She stood beside him awkwardly. She didn't want to invite him in but she didn't know what to say to him, either.

Saving her the trouble of deciding, he handed her a piece of paper. "That's my local cell phone number. You should memorize it."

She remembered the last time he'd given her his phone number. Her throat went tight, shades of a New Mexican sunrise coloring her thoughts. Her question came out without conscious thought. "You're staying here, then? In Austin?"

He didn't answer her directly. "I'll be near. For a while."

Their eyes spanned the distance between them, and for one crazy second—fulfilling the bad-date scenario—Alex imagined Gabriel kissing her. The idea was so unexpected, so ludicrous, that she found herself holding her breath. What would it be like to experience those cold lips pressing against her mouth, his fingers digging into her shoulders, his eyes drilling her own? Would it frighten her? Would it thrill her?

Would it do both?

Before she could carry the fantasy any further, Gabriel turned and disappeared down the stairs. Her thoughts in a jumble, Alex stepped inside and locked the door behind her.

Her elbow burned where he'd touched her.

CHAPTER SEVEN

THE FOLLOWING NIGHT, as Gabriel waited for the phone to ring, he stared out the window of his motel room. The view was of the parking lot but he didn't care, because he wasn't seeing the landscape. He was ten years in the past and back in New Mexico.

Weeks after the fiasco had finished, when he'd first found out about the old man's murder, Gabriel had put his fist through a wall, stunning the agents around him, everyone avoiding him for a while. The man's death had been totally useless, so pointless it had been insane.

The minute he'd heard about the violence, though, Gabriel had known René Cuvier was responsible. Guy Cuvier had surrounded himself with violent people; René, Guy's brother, was one of the worst. Cruel and crazy, he *liked* killing people. The last piece of the puzzle had fallen in place when Alex had revealed her stop at the station for directions. René must have known about her. He'd probably gone to the Missions' home either in between Alex's arrival but before Gabriel's and seen her bags, or he'd gone right after the Missions had left and seen the photo of the family. Either way, he'd then traced Alex's path into town, but he'd missed her.

If René *had* learned anything from the station attendant, it hadn't been enough, thank God. Gabriel hadn't been lying when he'd told Alex she'd be dead by now if the cartel had known more. The Agency couldn't have protected her all these years if that had been the case. Robert Mission had proved that point.

Gabriel cursed out loud. He should have quizzed Alex better that night, should have made sure she'd seen no one else, but he'd been too busy trying to figure out how in the hell things had gone so wrong so fast. The locals had dealt with the killing, and it'd gone down just as the Agency had wanted—as an unsolved murder.

Unsolved but not unpunished. Even though he hadn't been completely sure at that point, Gabriel had handled the problem.

But Alex would never know that. And it was only one of a hundred things she'd never know, the secrets too many, the bodies too deep.

But now, after all this time, someone was resurrecting the dead, following Alex, breaking into her apartment, planning who knew what... Clearly he'd missed someone, but who?

Gabriel closed his eyes and rubbed the lids with the back of his knuckles. Star bursts formed then disappeared as Alex's white face replaced them. When he'd taken her elbow, he hadn't been prepared for the sensations that had come with the connection. What was really strange was that she'd felt it, too. He had seen the same surprise in her eyes.

He'd recovered quickly, the facts making themselves heard like a shout within his brain. Even if Alex hadn't been who she was—even if they didn't share a history that no one knew—they could never share anything other than what they already did. She was too young and too vulnerable for him to even think about that way. He was on the downward swing of his life, but she still had time. Time she didn't need to spend with someone like him. As if that would ever happen anyway...

The phone rang, sparing him from further torture. Gabriel snatched it up, listened for a bit, then spoke. "At ten, I got it. You're close to the capitol, right? On Nueces Street?" He nodded and scribbled down an address, hanging up a second later without saying goodbye. Gabriel had one friend left at the Agency, a guy named Evan Frank. Evan would tell him what he could, but Gabriel had the feeling it wouldn't be much.

ON HIS WAY to meet Evan, Gabriel swung by Alex's apartment, but as he'd anticipated, her car was gone. He'd copied her date-book appointments when she'd been in Los Lobos and he knew she had planned more shopping with Ben Worthington's daughter, then a late dinner at the house with Ben. And Gabriel felt sure that was exactly what Alex was doing. The trip to Los Lobos notwithstanding, unplanned events had little place in her life. She now stuck to routine as fervently as she had indulged in self-destruction before.

Taking Guadalupe Street, Gabriel headed toward the capitol building, its glowing lights a beacon in the cold winter night. Within minutes he was on the right street and had located the proper address. An ordinary low-rise building with a nondescript sign and an innocuous list of tenants, the Agency's office looked just as Gabriel had expected. No one worked harder— or more successfully—to cloak their presence and their activities.

The lobby was deserted and silent. Neither Evan nor Gabriel had been anxious for anyone to know they were meeting, but they were even less eager for someone outside the Agency to see them together. By coming here they could at least control part of the situation.

Gabriel buzzed Evan's office and the elevator came to life. He stepped inside, and a few moments later, when the car opened to a floor that wasn't listed, he got off. Evan Frank waited for him just inside a set of double glass doors. Bulletproof doors.

More than a year and a half had passed since Gabriel had last seen the gangly agent, but he hadn't changed. Over six feet tall, with the legs and neck of a giraffe, Evan Frank was a detail man. He only had to hear or see something once; trivial *and* major facts then lodged inside his head to be available for later recall at any moment. Gabriel thought he was half computer.

They shook hands and exchanged a minimum of pleasantries. The knowledge took up so much of Evan's brain, his ability to make small talk was non-existent. Which was fine with Gabriel. He wasn't too great at it himself.

"This is about the Mission op," he said, sitting down in Evan's stark office a few minutes later. "Ten years ago in—"

"Los Lobos," the other man supplied, tapping a file on his desk. "Got it right here. Robert and Selena. Grown daughter, Alexis, son, Toby." He shook his head. "Bad situation."

Gabriel didn't bother to answer—everyone knew how things had gone down. "A problem's come up. Looks like someone might be harassing the daughter."

Evan's brown eyes blinked. "But you killed—"

Gabriel held up his hand. "I know who I *killed*." He paused. "I need to know who I left *alive*."

"Let me think about it." Evan turned away from Gabriel and put his feet against the wall, pushing his chair back so he could stare at the ceiling. From the marks on the paint, Gabriel gathered he did this frequently. After a second or two, he swung the chair around.

"Vail Villard."

He pronounced the name properly, his French as flawless as his memory.

"Who in the hell—"

"He was a friend of René Cuvier. A close friend. He's in Attica for two to three on charges totally unrelated to the Mission op."

"Then how could he be the one after Alex?"

The agent closed his eyes for a second, his lips moving as he obviously calculated something. When they popped open, he spoke. "He could have gotten out on October 15 of this year if he managed not to screw up."

Gabriel's face stayed immobile but his mind began to whirl. "Did we know about this jerk back then?"

"When the op was going down?" Evan shook his head. "No. It was later—after Guy Cuvier's family—the wife and daughter—had disappeared and René had been kil...died—that we tied the two of them together. By then we couldn't locate Villard."

Gabriel began to interrupt again, but Evan continued, knowing what he was going to ask. "The only reason I know where Villard is now is the NYC guys called me when they arrested him. So much time had passed since the other case had closed, I didn't bother to tell you. Actually, I'd forgotten about the guy. After everything went down, I'd flagged his name and never bothered to remove the note."

"Did you interview him?"

"I did," Evan replied. "He said he knew nothing and I couldn't press him. The details had already been sealed. More questions would have meant a court order and I didn't think it was worth it."

"How close were Villard and René Cuvier?"

"Very close. They were cousins by marriage. If Villard was somehow able to connect you to Cuvier's death and then back to the Missions..." Evan's jaw tightened. "It wouldn't be good, that's for sure."

Gabriel's voice turned grim. "Call NYC and find out if he's back on the street."

"That may take a while. It's late."

"I've been waiting ten years." Gabriel met the other man's now-troubled gaze. "I can last another hour."

Evan Frank turned without a word and hurried from his office, Gabriel listening to his muffled steps until a door opened and closed somewhere down the hallway. He reached for the file on the agent's desk, but as he picked it up, something fell out and fluttered to the carpet. Gabriel bent over quickly and retrieved the piece of paper.

It was the photograph of the Mission family he'd taken from her. Seeing Selena and Robert's brave and determined expressions brought everything back in a flood.

He hadn't known Robert even owned a gun, or Gabriel would never have let him go to the meeting that night. Cuvier had taken the computer disk from the scientist and had stuck it in his pocket. When his hand had come back out, he'd held a PK Walther. Robert had panicked and pulled out his own weapon.

Cuvier had planned Robert's death all along, but Robert had reacted in self-defense, pure and simple. Guy's family—and the rest of the cartel—didn't see it that way.

René had tracked down Robert six months later and murdered him. A few months after that, Gabriel had returned the favor. He didn't like to kill— René's ghost visited him, along with all the others—but in this case, Gabriel had known he'd done the right thing. He slipped the photograph into his wallet and put the file back on Evan Frank's desk. The Cuviers were scum and the world was better off without them.

So who was left?

The name Vail Villard meant nothing to Gabriel, but the man was most likely the one behind Alex's situation—there *was* no one else. Obviously René had known more than they'd suspected, if he'd followed her to the service station that night. Had he somehow told Villard before Gabriel had killed him? If that's what had happened, how had Vail located Alex? And why now? Gabriel's jaw tightened until it throbbed, a reaction he couldn't control.

He'd killed once to keep her safe. If he had to, he'd do it again.

ALEX PULLED AWAY from Ben's house with a lump in her throat. He'd had a rough day. When she and Libby had come back from the mall, they'd learned that Margaret had had to call Ben's private nurse. She usually came every other day, but he'd taken such a bad turn, Margaret had gotten scared. And rightly so. Alex was afraid he might not last much longer. He'd rallied enough to try to get her to stay for a late dinner, but Alex had declined. And then escaped. She couldn't handle seeing him like that.

With time on her hands and a restless energy, too, she turned the car toward the Y instead of home. The only way she could shake off the anxiety and guilt that had taken hold of her was to do some sort of physical activity. She wanted to think her feelings were associated with Ben, but she knew better. She'd been agitated and nervous ever since Gabriel had left her apartment.

She was frightened the killers knew more about her than Gabriel had thought, but she also felt awful knowing she was the cause of the station attendant's death. If she hadn't stopped there that night or if she'd just remembered and had told Gabriel, things would have been so different…

A thought that brought her back full circle to Gabriel. He was still hiding the truth from her. His secrecy bothered her, but her reaction to his presence disturbed her even more. The fantasy of kissing him had opened up a Pandora's box she'd never before considered. There were shadows in his eyes and mysteries behind his gaze. He was her enemy and her protector. He intrigued her yet repelled her.

How could one man offer sanctuary *and* danger?

Pulling into the parking lot, Alex put aside her thoughts. There was nothing she could do about them, and Gabriel would do what he wanted anyway, her own concerns irrelevant. Switching off the car, she suddenly noticed there were less than a dozen vehicles in the lot beside her own. Part of her wanted to turn back, but Alex forged on, pulling her gym bag out and heading for the glass doors, her pace quick against the cold wind. She flashed her membership card to the kid behind the desk, then within minutes she had on her suit. When she walked into the pool area, she suddenly stopped.

The huge space was completely empty of people, the sound of water slapping into the skimmer the only noise to break the eerie silence. She took two steps backward, even as she told herself she was being ridiculous. Did she really think someone could get past the front desk, make their way through the mazelike facility, find her and do her in? That was crazy—she was safe here. Then her thoughts were replaced by Gabriel's words.

"If they knew about you, we wouldn't be having this conversation. You'd already be dead."

Taking a deep breath, she put aside the worry along with her cover-up, walked to the edge of the pool and dived in. The water was the same cool temperature it usually was, and she slipped through the lane with strong, smooth strokes. Her mind blanked out everything as she glided soundlessly. Ten laps then ten more, her breath now coming in short spurts, her arms and legs beginning to ache. After a while, a glance at the clock behind the diving boards told her she'd been at it for twenty-five minutes and had almost done her mile. Ten more minutes and she was really hurting, fifteen more and she found herself clinging to the edge, her eyes closed, her lungs burning. The extra exertion felt good, the cleansing fire in her aching body a precursor, she hoped, to a calm night and restful sleep.

Then she heard something. A slithering sound, a whispered footstep.

Her eyes popped open. Through her goggles, she caught a glimpse of black boots poised on the coping. Before she could look up, a hand came down on her head.

Alex jerked in surprise and reached for the edge of the pool, but she reacted too late. Her fingers slipped off and her head went under. She began to flail, her arms and legs thrashing about in the water as terror took hold. She gasped, a lungful of water her only reward.

Grabbing her assailant's wrist, she fought, but her struggle was useless—the grip remained unyielding. The bitter sting of chlorine burned her throat and then her nose as she stared upward and blinked, her arms growing weak. Through her goggles, the watery shadow was a blur—she couldn't make out a single detail. Not wanting that sight to be her last, she squeezed her eyes shut.

Gabriel's face flashed before her and then she blacked out.

IT TOOK GABRIEL a minute to realize the irritating sound that was filling Evan's office was his own cell phone. He jerked the tiny phone from the clip at his waist and popped it open. "Yeah?"

The voice that answered him was hesitant. "Uh… I don't know who you are…but, uh, do you like…know someone named Alex Worthington?"

Gabriel sat up straight. "Who is this?"

The voice at the other end turned even more cautious. "This is Jason Noellert, at the Y. You, like, don't know me or anything…"

Gabriel jumped to his feet, his questions like bullets. "Then how in the hell did you get this number? Is Alexis there? Let me talk to her."

"I…I can't do that, man. That's why I'm calling. I found your number in her purse. She almost drowned. I wanted to call an ambulance or something but she freaked—''

Without waiting to hear more, Gabriel tore out of Evan's office, the phone still pressed to his ear. When he reached the door to the stairs, a surprised Evan called out his name from the end of the corridor but Gabriel kept going. Clattering down the staircase, he peppered the boy with more questions.

''Is she breathing?''

''Well, yeah, kinda.''

''Where are you?''

''We're at the YMCA—''

''Give me directions.''

The kid had obviously answered this question a thousand times. He rattled off the streets as Gabriel vaulted into his car and downshifted out of the parking lot on two wheels, the smell of burning rubber the only clue he'd ever been there.

WRAPPED IN A TOWEL, Alex lay beside the edge of the pool when Gabriel ran into the natatorium. Her lungs were screaming and her throat felt as if she'd swallowed acid, but she was alive, thank God...and Jason Noellert, she thought irreverently. If the kid hadn't come when he had, she would be dead.

She started to stand as Gabriel neared then realized she couldn't. Her legs were as watery as the rest of her. Her knees buckled and Gabriel rushed forward to catch her.

Easing her to the coping, he went down with her, his eyes furious. "What in the hell happened? I thought you were going shopping and then to dinner—"

Alex felt a catch in her chest that had nothing to do with the near drowning. How did he know everything about her life? The obvious answer—he'd been in her apartment again—made her shiver but she was too wiped out to do anything else. She started to answer him, then saw the boy standing behind them, his eyes still huge, his hands hanging awkwardly at his sides as if he didn't know what to do with them.

"I'm fine, Jason." Her voice was whiskey raw from the harsh water she'd swallowed, the words barely coming out. He didn't look convinced. "Really," she added painfully. "Please—don't worry about me. I'll be back tomorrow to tell your boss how wonderful you were. You saved my life."

He nodded but shot a glance at Gabriel as if relieved there was someone else around who could take the responsibility of Alex off his shoulders. He mumbled "You're welcome" then left the pool area, the door closing behind him with an echoing slam.

Alex turned back to Gabriel. His hands, she realized suddenly, were still on her arm, his eyes on her face.

"I'm all right," she repeated.

"You don't look all right. In fact, you look like

bloody hell. What stupid kind of balls-up happened here tonight, Alexis?''

His speech was thick with the accent she'd barely heard before, the use of her old name a slip she didn't miss.

"Someone tried to drown me," she said hoarsely.

"What the—" He uttered an obscenity, his fingers tightening before he broke off his words. "How in the hell did that happen? Did you see him? What—"

"I didn't get a good look." She interrupted him, her head tilting to the chair behind her where her goggles rested. "I had those on and I couldn't see. Whoever it was came up to the edge of the pool and surprised me, then pushed me down into the water." She swallowed, her throat aching with the effort.

"Why'd he stop?"

"Jason came in to lock up. I guess he heard him coming down the hallway."

"Did he see—"

She shook her head. "He was gone by the time Jason pushed the door open. He caught a glimpse as the guy went out the back but he was mainly interested in helping me."

Gabriel's jaw went into a sharp line, his voice harsh. "Are you sure you didn't see anything, Alex? Think hard. It's important—"

She frowned and looked down at his fingers—he

was hurting her. She raised a hand to pry away his grip, then her gaze fell to his feet.

She could see her reflection in the black boots he wore.

CHAPTER EIGHT

ALEX LURCHED to her feet, but she wasn't steady
enough to maintain her balance. Gabriel reached out
for her, catching her just before she stumbled backward into the pool.

"What the hell—"

She pulled away from him, her sudden, astonishing
fear crowding out her ability to breathe. She felt as if
she were drowning all over again, this time in dread
instead of water. "I—I…"

His fingers pressing into her arms, Gabriel held her
tightly, almost shaking her. They were inches apart.
If Gabriel couldn't hear her pulse pounding then he
could surely see her panic. She was flush with it,
overcome by it.

"What is it?"

"No—nothing."

He squeezed her forearms. "Tell me."

Her eyes couldn't leave his. She was trapped by
the heat emanating from them, the strength in his fingers. "Tell me," he ordered again. "What's wrong?"

The words came out, driven by an emotion she

didn't understand. "Yo-your boots," she sputtered. "You...you have on black boots. I saw black boots..."

His brow furrowed then cleared a moment later, the meaning of her stuttered exclamation coming to him. When he spoke, his assertion was a statement of fact not a question, his voice flat and unemotional. "You think I'm the one who just tried to drown you."

She didn't know what to say, but she didn't *have* to say anything. He'd said it all.

His hand still locked around her arm, Gabriel turned toward the door, dragging Alex behind him.

He let Alex stop long enough to get her purse from her locker then they went outside where Gabriel put her in a car she'd never seen before. The downtown streets were almost empty and Alex felt a corresponding vacancy inside her head. Strangely, her fear had fled, leaving nothing but a numbing coldness in its absence. Was there anything about this man she really understood? Who was he? *What* was he? Where was he taking her?

A few minutes later, Gabriel turned the car into the parking lot of a nondescript office building. Yanking a cell phone from his pocket, he punched out a number. Alex could hear a tinny voice at the other end. Gabriel spoke, his eyes connecting with hers across the front seat of the car.

"This is O'Rourke," he said. "I've got the girl

with me. I want you to look out the window and wave at her. Right now. Just do it.''

Alex could feel her legs trembling even though she was sitting down. Gabriel nodded toward the building. ''Go on,'' he said harshly. ''Look.''

She did as he commanded. Somewhere near the middle of the building, a man had parted a set of vertical blinds. He held a phone to his ear and waved down at her. She managed to get her own hand up but it took an immeasurable effort.

Gabriel spoke again. ''I'm handing her the phone. Tell her your name and who you are then tell her what you've been doing for the last hour and a half.''

Alex took the phone with a shaky hand and put it to her ear. ''Th-this is Alex Worthington.''

''I'm Evan Frank. I work with a governmental organization for which Mr. O'Rourke occasionally provides services.''

Clearly uncomfortable but unwilling to make Gabriel mad, the man spoke quickly, his voice awkward, his diction stilted. Alex cut her eyes to Gabriel's face. He was staring out the windshield of the car, his profile a granite mask.

''I understand.'' She hated the way she sounded, weak and afraid.

''Mr. O'Rourke and I have been talking. He was in my office from 10:00 p.m. until just about fifteen minutes ago. He left quickly after receiving a phone call. I have no idea where he went.''

"What were you talking about?"

"That's not something I can—"

Gabriel tore the phone out of Alex's fingers, cutting off the explanation before she could hear any more. He silenced her protest with a hard look.

"Did you hear anything back?" he asked. "All right. You can get me later when they do call. Use this number." He then quickly explained what had happened to Alex, issuing more instructions when he finished. "Call the Austin P.D. and take care of this. I'm sure the Y will file a report and we don't need that right now." He flipped the phone shut then looked at Alex. "Are you satisfied?"

She didn't know if she was or not, but she didn't have another choice. Too aware of their isolation in the darkened parking lot to do anything else, Alex nodded.

Gabriel threw the car into gear and they left. Again, she had no idea where he was taking her, but the adrenaline that had powered Alex this far suddenly drained from her body, leaving her limp and nauseous. Closing her eyes against her roiling stomach, she gripped the door handle and prayed she wouldn't throw up. She felt Gabriel put his coat over her. The rest of the drive was a blank.

GABRIEL FOLLOWED another car through the gates and into Alex's apartment complex, parking as close to her unit as he could. As he went to Alex's side of the car, he glanced around but thankfully saw no one. It might be hard to explain her appearance at the moment; she was wearing a bathing suit and a leather jacket. Not to mention the fact that she still seemed pretty shaky. He helped her out of the car and up the stairs, but halfway there she began to totter. Pulling her into his arms, Gabriel carried her the rest of the way. Once inside, Gabriel strode through the apartment with Alex still in his arms, stripes of light following him down the narrow hallway and into her bedroom where he placed her on the bed. Her blond hair twisted into damp strings across the pillowcase as her eyes stared up at him. They were so hollowed and empty, he immediately felt a corresponding reaction.

He should have pulled back but he couldn't.

He reached toward her face and the smooth, white skin of her cheek. She watched him without protest and then he was touching her, the back of his finger tracing an imaginary line down her jaw to her chin and then to her neck. At the base of her throat, he could feel her pulse beneath his fingertip. It was ragged and fast. Too fast.

"Did you really think I would try to kill you?" His whisper hovered between them.

"I didn't know. I saw the boots.... I was scared...."

"I'm here to help you, Alexis. Nothing more."

"Why do you care?"

He lifted his finger from her neck and put his hands on either side of where she rested, the pillows compressing beneath his weight. Answering that question was the one thing he would never do. She hated him enough already. If she knew all he had seen—all he had *done*—she'd never absolve him. But she was too smart and too quick. She'd become a survivor and lying was no longer one of his options. He had to tell her something.

But for just an instant, he wanted to kiss her instead and his gaze fell to her lips. They were sensual and fuller than they should have been, achingly beautiful. He raised his eyes back to hers where she read his intention as if he'd spoken it aloud. She stayed where she was, surprising him. The thought crossed his mind that she wanted—needed—the contact between them.

He gave her face a final glance then he slowly stood. Her expression now hidden by a band of darkness, he sensed disappointment—but it was his own, he told himself—not hers.

"Why?" she whispered.

For one startled moment he thought she was asking him why he'd moved away, then he understood.

"I care because...I gave someone a promise to watch over you."

"Who?"

"Your father," he said quietly. "And your mother, too."

Her expression changed swiftly and she pulled herself up in the bed, clutching his jacket to her shoulders. "Tell me more."

"There isn't more to tell. When I got to the scene they were still alive. They asked me to keep an eye on you. That's it."

She made a sound of frustration. "That can't be 'it.' I want to move on, but I can't when the past is holding me back. I have to know more about what happened, Gabriel. I *have* to."

It was the first time he could ever remember her saying his name. He didn't like the way it sounded falling from her lips; it made him want things he couldn't have.

"The past doesn't hold us back, Alex. We do that to ourselves."

"That's easy for you to say—"

"No." He spoke with his father's condemning voice ringing in his ears. "It's not easy for anyone. We all have anchors we're dragging. You, me, the guy next door." He jerked his thumb toward the darkened street. "You might not recognize their problems like you do your own, but believe me, they're there."

"Then you should understand even better." She climbed across the bed to be closer to where he stood. "You can help me cut my anchor. You're the *only* one who can do that."

He started to answer but she reached out and took his hand in hers. Her slender fingers were cold—from the near drowning or nerves, he didn't know. Her eyes pleaded with him.

"You can help me, Gabriel. You can tell me what really happened that night. That's all I want, all I'll ever ask. I'll disappear and you'll never have to deal with me again, I promise."

"That's impossible."

"No, it's not! I've done it before and I can do it again. I'll find a new place to live and get a new name and—"

He pulled his hand away, her touch too compelling, her gaze too urgent.

"I promise you, Gabriel. I promise…"

"You can't make that kind of commitment, Alexis…" He looked down at her and shook his head slowly. "Dead people can't keep promises."

Too stunned to do anything else, Alex watched Gabriel leave the bedroom. A moment later she heard him searching through the cabinets in the kitchen, then running the can opener and the microwave. The smell of chicken noodle soup wafted down the hall and she felt like throwing up.

How could he do this to her? How could he keep the truth behind his eyes, doling out bits when it pleased him? Hating the way she'd pleaded with him, she'd felt as if she had no other option. He held all the cards. Would she never be free from this nightmare?

She lay back down on the bed and closed her eyes, Gabriel's face swimming inches from her own as it had a few minutes before. She wasn't sure which was worse—knowing he knew her secrets or knowing he'd wanted to kiss her.

The answer was neither. The worst thing was knowing *she* had wanted him.

The realization shook her, and she remembered the first time she'd seen him. His mouth had seemed cruel then. The line was no less harsh or threatening now, but God, she'd longed to taste it. How could she feel that way when an hour before she'd thought he was trying to kill her?

Her confusion grew and took on a dimension of its own. She desperately wanted his help but he wasn't going to give it to her, not in the way she needed it. Her crazy thoughts seesawed. One minute she was willing to do anything to get him to open up, and the next, all she could do was wish to God he'd simply go away. Burying her face into her pillow, she moaned.

Five minutes later, carrying a tray, Gabriel came back into the bedroom. "I heated some soup. You need to get something down."

She rolled over. "I'm not hung—"

"I don't care if you're hungry or not." He set the tray beside her and flipped on the bedside lamp. "You need to eat."

Arguing was pointless. Alex picked up the spoon

and dipped it into the soup. Gabriel waited to make sure she ate then he walked to the window, cradling a mug in his hands. He stared out for a moment before reaching up and shutting the blinds. Eating like a robot, Alex continued to mull over the situation until a new thought hit her. Maybe…just maybe…

"Why do you do that all the time?" Lifting the spoon, she indicated the window, her voice casual as she tried to come up with a way to broach the subject she wanted to discuss. "Look out like that?"

His answer was cryptic as he moved away from the window. "Somebody needs to."

She couldn't have asked for a more perfect opening.

"Somebody like Evan Frank?" she asked in an innocent voice.

Gabriel stared at her and didn't answer.

"He told me he worked for a government agency that occasionally uses your 'services.' Is it the same agency you worked for when I met you?"

"Yes."

"So that's how you knew when I called you?"

"Yes. I stay in touch with them. They call me when they need me."

"Who are these people?" She stopped him before he could answer. "And don't flash a phony ID at me and think it'll work again. I want to know the truth this time. Tell me who they are."

He looked at her wearily, his jaws shadowed by a developing beard. "Don't ask me that."

Ignoring his warning, Alex forged ahead. "Evan Frank still works for them, right? And that's *where* he works? In that office building where we went?"

"Dammit to hell, Alex, you can't go there." Gabriel had been leaning against her bedroom wall, but as she spoke, he straightened, his voice sharp. "Don't even think about it."

"Why not? If you won't help me, then maybe he will."

"He can't and he won't, so forget about it. It'd be a waste of time anyway. You wouldn't even be able to find him."

Her laugh was hollow. "What? You going to tell me now the building won't be there when I go back?"

"No. That's not what I'm saying." Each word was deliberate, cold. "Just trust me for a change. You won't be able to locate him."

"But he's helping you."

"That's right—he's helping me. But he won't help you."

His answers were more frustrating than his silence. Alex gave up—for the moment—and returned to her soup. Gabriel's cell phone chirped a few minutes later.

"THEY'RE HAVING PROBLEMS with their mainframe." Evan Frank explained the computer glitch in detail, but none of the conversation made sense to Gabriel.

He could have blamed his confusion on his lack of computer literacy but the truth was much closer—it rested, in fact, in a bed down the hall where a blonde with troubled eyes was waiting.

"Can't you phone the jail, for God's sake?" Gabriel interrupted the long-winded agent. "I need to know if Villard is out, dammit!"

"That's what I just explained, Gabriel." Evan sounded as exasperated as Gabriel. "The phone lines are out…therefore the computer is out…therefore I can get no information until everything is up and running again. What part of that don't you understand?"

"They don't have a backup system? What the hell kind of—"

"Of course they have a backup," Frank interrupted. "But they're not going to use it to process our query. They have too much other stuff going on right now. I've been told they'll get to it when they can, which means don't call us, we'll call you."

"All right, all right…" Gabriel rubbed his forehead. "But you phone me the minute you learn anything. It's important."

"I understand and I promise I will—" The rest of Frank's reassurance went unheard. Gabriel had already punched the end button, the conversation over.

What in the hell was he going to do now?

He turned and stared down the hallway, the sound

of running water coming toward him. Steam followed a moment later. Alex was taking a shower. He thought of her standing under the hot water, rivulets running down her body.

Pivoting, he went back into the kitchen and poured another two fingers of tequila into his coffee mug. Seeing Alex on the side of that pool, her face pale, her eyes scared, had been more unnerving than Gabriel could have ever imagined. Not to mention the fact that she'd thought he was the one who'd tried to kill her... He'd grabbed the first bottle in her liquor cabinet his hand had touched, knocking back as much as he could while her soup had heated.

He drank slower now but he was still rattled, maybe even more so. The shit was piling up. Villard could be out there somewhere, God only knew what in the hell was going on, and to top it all off, Gabriel couldn't believe how desperately he'd wanted to kiss Alex. The urge—no, the *need*—had almost won out over the remaining bit of common sense he had left. He'd battled himself and won, but if he'd lost...he didn't even want to think about that possibility.

The sound of running water stopped. He headed back into the living room, his mug in hand, and looked out over the parking lot, remembering Alex's question about his vigilance. Everything seemed quiet. Closing the blinds, he turned on a lamp then sat down in the chair beside the sofa, his body suddenly rebelling against the way he'd treated it for the past week and a half. His eyelids drooped, then a few moments later he sensed Alex's presence.

"Did you get anything to eat?"

He opened his eyes. She wore a thick white terry-cloth robe with a collar and rolled-up sleeves. It covered her from her neck to her toes. She'd scrubbed her face, and her hair hung in wet ribbons around it. She looked exhausted and scared and incredibly sexy.

He held up the coffee mug and thickened his accent. "I'm drinking my dinner. It's an auld tradition in my family..."

She said nothing, moving instead to sit down on the couch beside him. He caught the scent of her soap. "Did you eat your soup?" he asked. The question was a distraction. For himself, not her.

She nodded. "Thank you for fixing it for me."

"You're welcome."

The conversation had the stilted tone that strangers used, which was, Gabriel reasoned, probably the right one. They *were* strangers. Intimate strangers.

"How do you feel?" he asked. "I've got a doctor I can call if you need to see someone."

"I'm all right but thanks for the offer. Thanks for...for taking care of me, too. If you want to go now, that's fine."

He sipped his drink, then carefully put down the mug on the coffee table between them. "I'm not going anywhere," he said. "I'm not going to leave you alone."

They looked at each other, the warm light of the lamp falling between them, uniting their shadows. She started to protest, but he held up his hand, his voice was as weary as his body.

"I don't know what we're dealing with here, Alex. It could be some nut who has it in for you—a student or maybe somebody off the street, who knows—or it could be something more serious. Something connected to the past. Until I figure this out, I'm not leaving. And you shouldn't want me to, either."

"But I'm sure I'll be safe—"

"Why? What makes you so sure?"

She raised a hand and indicated the door. "I have locks. There's a guard…"

"Oh, right," he said. "The locks a monkey could pick and the guard we never saw last night—I forgot about them."

"I could call the police," she said defensively.

"And tell them what?"

His question silenced her. She dropped her head and he let her absorb his words before speaking quietly. "I'm the only thing you've got, Alex. I'm all there is between you and whoever's out there. Whether you like it or not, I'm going to stay here. I can't leave you alone."

She raised her gaze. "I've been alone for ten years. I can handle this, whatever it is."

"Not if it's connected to your past. These people aren't the kind you can handle."

"But *you* can?"

"I can...and I have."

After a long moment—long enough for him to wonder what he would do should she refuse—Alex nodded, albeit reluctantly. "All right," she conceded. "But just for tonight. That's it."

"Of course," he lied, looking straight into her eyes. "Just for tonight. I promise."

ALEX MADE UP the couch then disappeared into her bedroom. Knowing Gabriel was in her apartment, knowing he was right down the hallway, should have made her relax. After all, someone had just tried to kill her... He was right—she *should* be grateful he'd refused to leave her alone.

But she wasn't. She was more nervous and edgy than ever before, her mind going over and over who could possibly hate her enough to drown her. The list was short—no, nonexistent. She couldn't think of a single person, including Gabriel. He had no good reason to want her dead and she'd been crazier than usual to even consider that a possibility.

Giving up after an hour, she finally accepted the fact that she was not going to get any rest. Compounding her problem, the longer she lay in the bed, the more her bruises and sore spots made themselves known.

She rose from the twisted covers and headed for the kitchen. She kept her aspirin in the cabinet by the sink. The pills wouldn't do anything for her overactive mind, but maybe they would help her aching body.

She moved as soundlessly as possible but she shouldn't have bothered. Gabriel was awake. When she emerged from the tiny kitchen, his disembodied voice came to her from out of the darkness. "Trouble sleeping?"

She stopped. "All that thrashing around must have sent me into the edge of the pool. My muscles are complaining." She rubbed her shoulder and winced. "I took some aspirin."

"Do you want something stronger? I can get it if you do."

"Doctors who make house calls? Twenty-four-hour pharmacies? New identities... Is there anything you don't have access to?"

He shrugged. "I do what I can."

Alex gingerly kneaded her upper arm, a long-lost memory suddenly coming to her. "What I really need is some Magic cream."

"Magic cream?" He sounded skeptical.

She nodded. "When I was a kid and I'd hurt myself in some way—real or not—my mom would always bring out her 'magic cream.' It came in a blue jar and it smelled like gardenias. She'd rub it on my knee or elbow or whatever I'd thought I'd injured and the pain would disappear...like magic."

"Definitely better than anything I could produce."

Alex agreed then said, "I figured out when I was ten that it was only her skin cream, but I never told her I knew. When I went to Peru, she gave me a jar of it."

Gabriel said nothing, and Alex fell silent, too, a sudden uncomfortable link forming between them. It felt strange to share this tidbit, almost as if she was doing something forbidden. She looked across the room. All she could see of Gabriel was his silhouette.

"Did you need magic cream in Peru?" he asked after a moment.

"I could have used an ocean of it, but I'm not sure even that could have helped the situation."

"What happened?"

"What didn't? I went there to live with someone who turned out to be a much different person than I thought he was. The whole thing was a disaster. My mom and dad had warned me, but I didn't listen."

He waited a bit then he surprised her, a rueful smile lifting his lips. The expression transformed his face for a heartbeat. "Where's the magic cream store? Maybe we should go buy some."

She smiled briefly in return, then her voice went soft as she shook her head. "It wouldn't be magic if we bought it. It'd just be cream…that smelled like gardenias."

He didn't answer, but she knew he understood.

She let the darkness wrap around her for a bit, and then she spoke again, almost as an afterthought. "I smelled her perfume the other night. When I came in and couldn't find my sketch. The scent came to me suddenly and then it was gone.''

He stayed as he was, motionless on the couch. ''That's not possible.''

''I know,'' she said. ''I told myself that. But it didn't feel impossible at the time. The fragrance of gardenias filled my bathroom when the heat came on. I could have sworn it.''

''You must have smelled something else.''

She shook her head. ''No...no. I'd recognize the perfume anywhere, anytime.''

''Then you were imagining it. Our senses can manufacture impressions, send us false signals, especially when we're frightened.''

''I guess that's what I did. There isn't any other explanation for it,'' she said. ''There can't be.''

''You're right,'' he agreed. ''There can't be.''

She waited for him to say something else, but he stayed silent. After a second, she went back down the hall and climbed in bed. But she didn't sleep. Her eyes wide open, her mind swirling, she thought about the man in her darkened living room.

She was out of magic cream and there was really only one path she could take, because Gabriel wasn't going to help her. She had to get rid of him and do this her way, on her terms.

The realization left her feeling empty and alone.

CHAPTER NINE

GABRIEL HAD COFFEE made and a second batch of pancakes cooked by the time Alex's alarm sounded the following morning. He'd gotten up early, experience telling him it was useless to try to sleep after they'd talked the second time. Alex's revelation that she'd smelled Selena's perfume the night the sketch went missing had sent his thoughts in a direction he didn't like. He'd always assumed Selena would never do anything to put her daughter in danger—not after all the sacrifices she and Robert had made to keep the children safe—but anything was possible. He thought about the white Lexus, then shook his head. He didn't doubt that Alex had recognized the scent, but it couldn't have come from Selena. No way.

He broke off in midthought when Alex entered the kitchen. Her eyes went to the stove and then the coffeepot before coming back to him.

He pointed with the plastic spatula in his hand to the table in the corner.

"Sit down. The pancakes are almost ready." He

turned back to the range. "How do you feel this morning?"

"Okay," she said, taking a chair. "But sore. And my throat's still raw."

He filled a plate and put it before her, then fixed a mug of coffee and handed it to her as well.

She thanked him and picked up her fork, but when he stayed by the counter, leaning against the Formica, she stopped her hand in midflight. "You aren't going to eat?"

"I already have," he said. "I've been up a while."

She ate in silence as he watched. After she'd cleaned her plate and he'd poured them both more coffee, Gabriel spoke carefully. He had to approach her in just the right way—he was beginning to realize this situation had the same potential for catastrophe as the night ten years earlier. "I'll take you to get your car when you're done. I want to—"

She started shaking her head before he'd even finished. "I can call a cab."

He put down his mug and looked at her. "I need to find the kid who pulled you out last night. I have to talk to him."

"I can do that."

"You won't ask him the right questions."

Her expression shifted and he read her thoughts before she could speak. "You're a smart woman, Alex, so why are you doing this?"

"Doing what?"

"Acting as if you don't want my help."

"I'm not acting." Standing up, she took her plate and mug to the sink, brushing past him as she did so. She put the dishes down with a clatter then turned to face him. They were standing so close he could see the texture of her skin, the curl of her eyelashes. She wore a look of determination that told him she'd carefully considered what she was about to say.

"I *don't* want your help, because you're not going to give it to me. You do things your way and to hell with everyone else. To top it off, I don't trust you."

She had every right to those emotions and more. That didn't change a thing for Gabriel, though. "I'm all you've got," he said.

"That's what you told me last night," she said. "But that's not the truth. I've got what I've had for the past ten years and that's myself."

"You don't understand—"

She flared at him. "I understand more than you think, okay? I know you know what happened that night, and I know you're not going to tell me. Ever. How do you think that makes me feel? You know more about my past than I know myself!"

"That's not important—"

"Yes, it is! I think about it every hour of the day, dammit! I can't *stop* thinking about it. My whole family died and I don't even know why." She struggled to keep herself in check. "All I want to know is why... Just why, that's it. But you're never going to tell me, and what's more, you're going to stand in my way so I can't find out on my own."

If she'd been anyone else, Gabriel would have walked away and never looked back. But she wasn't. She was Alex and, dammit to hell, he understood her anger, her sense of loss, her past. He understood because he was responsible for it all. He did the only thing he could think of—he reached out and took her into his arms.

ALEX WANTED to resist but she couldn't. The shock of Gabriel's embrace was immediately overcome by an overwhelming need. She couldn't remember the last time a man had held her, the last time she'd felt this way. Maybe she never had, she thought with a jolt. Tightening his arms, Gabriel brushed her temple with his lips, his breath warm and soft as he murmured meaningless reassurances. She felt as if she'd found something she hadn't even known she was searching for.

The shock was too much. Last night, she'd made up her mind to send Gabriel away. Now she was in his arms.

She put her hands against his chest and pushed him back. He stayed where he was for a second, then he relented. "It's okay," he said softly.

"No, it's not." She lifted her gaze to his. His dark eyes were full of the same shadows she had in her heart. "It's not okay. Not at all. And it never will be unless you tell me more."

"There's nothing else I can say, Alex. Not at this point. It would be too dangerous."

Like the smallest spark of a tiny fire, hope flared. "Not at this point? As opposed to not ever?"

His reluctant expression told her he wished he hadn't spoken, but he had, so now he was forced to deal with it. "I have to figure out what's going on. Then we'll see."

Her resolution from the night before came back to her swiftly. "No," she said with determination. "I don't want a 'we'll see.' I want a promise. When the time is right, you have to tell me what you know."

"I can't do that."

"Then leave." She pointed behind to the door. "Right now. Get out."

GABRIEL KEPT HIS FACE expressionless, but he felt a wave of anger at her attempt to manipulate him—that was how *he* handled things, not Alex. "This is stupid," he said. "You want to trade your life for information."

"There are worse things than being dead."

"You don't know what you're saying."

"I know *exactly* what I'm saying." She paused. "And I don't care." Her eyes were steady and calm, and in a flash he understood.

She *was* telling him the truth, not trying to control

him. She really didn't care. Unbidden, his gaze went
to her bracelets. Death *didn't* scare her: They were
actually old friends.

But Gabriel had to fulfill the pledge he'd made to
Robert Mission or he'd become the kind of man his
father had been. A cruel son of a bitch who believed
in nothing but himself. Besides, Gabriel wouldn't put
it past Alex to simply leave, either. She was a curious
mix of fearlessness and vulnerability—she might decide to do this on her own. Deep down, there was a
third, even stronger, reason, too. Gabriel couldn't give
it voice, but it was there just the same. In her hazel
eyes. In the curve of her shoulder. In the hollow of
her neck.

What was one more lie if it kept her safe?

"All right," he said quietly. "I'll tell you what I
can *when* I can..."

She didn't miss the unspoken word at the end of
his agreement. Her expression became guarded.
"But?" she said for him.

"I want to stay here." He pointed to the floor.
"Until this thing is resolved."

His demand was clearly not what she'd expected.
Surprise crossed her face, and her fingers flew to her
throat. He wondered for a moment what she'd thought
he was going to ask for. "You want to move in with
me?"

"It won't be forever."

They exchanged a long look, too many issues flying between them to even be expressed, some too dangerous to *ever* be spoken. After a moment, she nodded and the decision was made.

ALEX HEADED to the back of the apartment for her coat, feeling Gabriel's eyes on her every step of the way. He said nothing when she returned, and the trip to the YMCA was equally silent. Which was fine with her. She needed time to digest what he'd said and even more time to think about what had happened between the two of them. Finding herself in Gabriel's arms wasn't the last thing she'd expected—not after he'd put her down in the bed last night—but her reaction to his touch had taken her completely by surprise.

And now she'd agreed to let him stay with her until the situation was resolved.

At the Y, he parked next to her car, then they walked together to the building, a cold winter wind buffeting their steps. A norther had blown in overnight, the sky now gray and holding the smell of sleet. Opening the door for her to enter first, Gabriel glanced at her as she passed him, their eyes meeting.

Alex shivered but not because of the dropping temperature. With their new arrangement, their relationship had taken a step in a much different direction. She should have felt much safer with Gabriel so close, but that wasn't the case. Suddenly her world felt more dangerous than ever.

The receptionist called the supervisor to the front, eyeing Alex as she spoke into the intercom system. Obviously the story of her near drowning had already gotten around. A few moments later, a woman stepped into the lobby. She wasn't much older than the kid who'd helped Alex last night. With a friendly but cautious demeanor, she held out her hand and introduced herself as Janice Holt.

Alex was effusive in her thanks and Gabriel was charming, but the young manager didn't completely relax until Alex reassured her she didn't blame the facility for any lack in security.

"Jason was wonderful," Alex said. "If he hadn't come along when he did, I'm afraid things might have ended a different way."

"That's what the police said. Have they contacted you yet?"

Gabriel and Alex exchanged a quick look. "No," Alex said. "They haven't, but I'm sure—"

"As soon as Jason called and told me what had happened, I contacted them," the woman replied. "You had already left, but they took the report."

"I turned the phone off last night," Gabriel said smoothly, "or I'm sure they would have called. Alex needed her rest."

The woman nodded, her expression now sympathetic.

"We'd like to contact Jason and thank him again. Is he here?"

"He doesn't come on shift until later tonight. I'm sure you can catch him at home, though. He lives right behind here in a huge apartment complex. You can't miss it. He's in 708."

Gabriel smiled warmly. "That's great. Thank you so much."

She blushed then accompanied Alex to the back to pick up her things she'd left the night before. When they returned to the lobby a few moments later, Gabriel stood by the front door, waiting. Alex shook the woman's hand once more and promised that she'd return. Ten minutes after that, they located the complex and then the apartment.

"You wait here," Gabriel said as Alex started out of the car. "I can do this better alone."

She started to argue then stopped. Gabriel was probably right—the boy would open up more without her there. She nodded unhappily, watching as he exited the car and crossed the parking lot to knock on the door. It opened so quickly, Alex wondered if Janice Holt had called and warned the teenager they were coming. If he had known, it didn't seem to matter. He let Gabriel in and closed the door behind him. Fifteen minutes passed, then Gabriel came back out.

"What'd he say?" she asked as Gabriel climbed back into the Toyota.

"Not much." His voice was tight with frustration. "Just like you said, he caught a glimpse of the person who attacked you but that's all—just a glimpse.

Dressed in black, not too tall, not too fat...nothing but average. Couldn't even say for certain if it was a male or female. Whoever it was found an unlocked door in the back leading to the alley, but Jason couldn't tell if it was picked or accidentally left open."

Leaning to one side, Gabriel reached into his pocket and pulled something out. "He did show me this, though. Said he found it on the steps outside this morning. I slipped him twenty dollars and he gave it to me."

Alex took the thin gold bracelet from Gabriel's fingers and held it up to the light. The clasp was broken and hanging off, but that wasn't what caught her eye. She studied the gold a bit longer, then her gaze went past the piece of jewelry to the man sitting beside her. Reading her expression, he nodded once. He'd seen what she'd seen.

A single blond hair was caught in one of the links.

GABRIEL OPENED the door to Alex's apartment, the tiny wire he'd placed against the doorjamb when they'd left still intact. He quickly checked out the apartment anyway. No one had been inside. He came back to the entry and nodded to Alex just as his cell phone rang.

"Villard's not in prison anymore," Evan Frank said with no preamble. "They opened the doors last month and he slithered away."

"Shit!" From across the room, where Alex was removing her coat, she turned and stared. He waved her attention off, pivoting away from her curious look. "Where's he living?"

"In a halfway house in New Jersey. At least that's where they sent him."

"Get somebody over there," Gabriel instructed, his voice low. "Make sure he's actually there. I want an eyewitness, Frank. A real live person to tell me he's seen him living there and working there or doing whatever in the hell it is he's doing. Understand?"

"I'm on it."

"And Evan...one more thing—"

"Yeah?"

"I've got a piece of jewelry I need examined."

"Marybeth's still down the hall."

"Good." Marybeth Allister was the Agency's resident expert on gold and jewelry. She could look at a ring and five minutes later tell what year it'd been made, where it'd come from, hell, who the last person was that had worn it.

"I'll be there later." Almost as an afterthought, Gabriel added. "I'll need some DNA work done, too."

The agent sighed. "We'll be here."

Gabriel snapped the phone shut and cursed again. Having Villard to worry about was the last thing he needed.

"What is it?"

Glancing to where Alex stood, Gabriel knew he
had to explain. Alex wasn't going to let him off and
he might lose her entirely if he didn't give her something.

"I had Frank checking on something for me. He
had news and it wasn't good."

She waited.

"A man I didn't want to be walking around is now
out of prison," he said. "We need to make sure he's
not in the area."

"Who is he?"

"Who he is isn't important. Who he's connected
to matters."

"He knew my parents?"

"No, but he was close to someone who did. He
might...be useful to talk to."

She nodded once, then walked down the hall without saying another thing, disappearing into her studio.
She'd taken him at his word. He'd said he would tell
her what he could, when he could...and she believed
him. He felt hollow inside. His lies were beginning
to bury him.

A moment later, the phone rang. He heard her answer it, and her voice muted, but not before he figured
out that Ben Worthington's daughter was on the other
end.

When the conversation finished, Gabriel went to
the doorway of the bedroom. Wearing a white apron
over her clothing, Alex stood in front of the window,

facing him, a canvas on an easel before her. He wondered what she was painting.

"Libby's coming over," Alex said. "Have you decided how we're going to explain your presence?"

Waiting for his answer, she dipped her brush then drew it carefully across the canvas.

"I've got to go see Evan," he answered. "When she gets here, I'll leave. You won't have to explain anything."

"That'll work for now," she agreed. "But what about later? People are bound to ask."

"Just tell them I'm a friend. That's all they need to know."

"A friend who's visiting for a while?" She wiped the bristles on a stained rag at her side.

"That sounds reasonable to me."

She continued to clean the brush. "How good a friend?"

The undercurrents suddenly turned swift and deep. "That depends, doesn't it?"

She lifted her eyes. "On what?"

"On you." He waited a moment. "How many 'close' friends do you have at the moment?"

"None."

"Would Libby think it unusual?"

"I'm not sure," she said. "I've dated since divorcing her father, but there's been no one special. Certainly no one living here with me."

"Then maybe it's time."

She layered more paint on her brush and eased it across the canvas. Finally, she nodded. Gabriel didn't know whether to be relieved or more worried than before.

CHAPTER TEN

WHEN LIBBY RANG the doorbell half an hour later, Alex was still shaking. There was something building between her and Gabriel that she didn't understand, a pressure she wasn't sure they could contain.

Still holding the paintbrush she'd been using, she started down the hall to open the door, but Gabriel beat her to it. Libby stepped inside just as Alex reached the living room, the young woman sending Alex a bright smile and Gabriel a puzzled look.

"You must be Libby," he said, his accent completely gone. "It's nice to meet you. Alex has told me a lot about you." He held out his hand in a smooth and polished way. "I'm Gabriel O'Rourke, an old friend of Alex's."

Libby gaped, they shook hands, then Gabriel stepped back to where Alex waited. Putting his arm around her waist, he looked down and smiled slowly at her, sensually, Alex realized with a start.

"You didn't tell me she was so beautiful," he said with a nod in Libby's direction. "I heard talented and smart, but not gorgeous."

His hand weighed heavily on her hip, his body giving off a heated energy. "I did tell you," she said, contradicting him for reasons she couldn't explain. "You must not have been listening…"

He drew Alex closer and leaned down to brush his mouth against her temple. "I guess I *wasn't* paying attention." He smiled at Alex. "I had something else on my mind last night."

His soft-as-rain voice flowed over Alex, the sexual nuance so real that for a moment she thought him serious. Then she remembered. She stiffened and tried to pull away, but he wouldn't let her, his fingers holding her fast.

Libby spoke quickly. "You should have told me you had company, Alex. I didn't need to come over now—"

"It's fine," Alex said, her voice as relaxed as she could make it, which wasn't very much, standing so close to Gabriel. "Gabriel's on his way out anyway."

"I have some Christmas shopping to do." Raising one dark eyebrow, he acted mysterious. "Something sparkly, I think…" He released Alex—finally!—and walked across the room to lift his black leather coat from the couch.

Libby's gaze followed him and Alex looked on, the young girl's response to Gabriel something Alex had seen before in women near him. The manager at the club had reacted the same way, her manner growing animated, her eyes bright. There *was* something about him, she admitted to herself. Something intense, something dark, something that dragged her ever closer toward him when she should be running the other way.

"I won't be gone too long," he said. "We're going to La Fonda tonight, right?"

She kept the surprise from her voice, but just barely. How on earth did he know about La Fonda? "If that's what you want," Alex answered.

"I do," he said. He held her stare for a bit longer, then he came to where she waited, bringing her body against his to kiss her. It wasn't a quick-peck-see-you-later kind of kiss. It was a this-will-last-but-only-until-I-get-back kind of kiss. When finally he raised his head, she was breathless. He touched her cheek with his finger, then nodded to Libby. "We'll see you again, I hope, before the holidays?"

She nodded. "Of course..."

The door closed behind him a moment later, the air going out with him, both women frozen in place, Alex by his kiss, Libby by his charm.

"Oh. My. God." Libby found her voice and turned back to Alex. "Why on earth didn't you tell me about him? How long have you been going out? Where's he from? What's he do?" She waited breathlessly for Alex's answers, dropping her purse on the nearby table.

"He's...a very old fr-friend," Alex stuttered. "I've

known him forever. Even—even before I knew your father. Long before,'' she improvised.

"And he's back in your life.'' Libby sighed, a romantic fantasy clearly building. "And you're desperately in love…''

"Oh, Libby, I don't—'' Alex broke off, imagining what Gabriel would say. "I don't know about that,'' she finished lamely.

"What's not to know?'' Libby said with astonishment. "He's obviously in love with you. A blind man could have seen that!''

Alex dropped her paintbrush, then leaned over, her fingers grabbing the wooden handle as she gave herself time to form an answer. Their act had obviously been too good. Sure, Alex felt some perverse attraction to him, but only in a dangerous kind of way. And if he felt anything, it was purely hormone driven, nothing else. Alex straightened. "Libby, sweetie, I think you're dreaming…''

"No, I'm not,'' the young girl said in a very adult voice. "He's in love with you.''

"You're confused. It's not what you think—''

Her expression turned serious. "I've only seen one other man stare at you like that, Alex. And I *know* how he feels.'' She shook her head. "I'd recognize that look anywhere. Daddy still loves you…and this man does, too.''

JUST AS Evan Frank had done, Marybeth Allister met Gabriel at the elevator. The agent pumped Gabriel's hand, her grip firm and dry. There were very few women at the Agency—the lifestyle was nomadic and ties were discouraged—but that hadn't fazed Marybeth. Her lover was a reporter for an international television news agency. They met when they could in some exotic locale, spent a few days, then went their separate ways again. Plainspoken and unflappable, she was an excellent agent, in the field and in the office. No one knew the gold trade better.

"I hear the Mission op has raised its ugly head again." Gabriel trailed behind her as they headed for her lab. She sent him a glance over her shoulder. "How'd you get pulled into that deal a second time?"

"It's a long story," he said. "And getting longer. I'll buy you a drink when this is over and give you all the details."

She laughed. "Just one? Must not be too bad if a single will cover it."

He thought of the woman he'd just left, of the ghosts in her past and the grief in her eyes. He thought about her lips. "You're right," he conceded. "We'll probably have to close down the place..."

They turned a corner and went into Marybeth's lab. Servicing the FBI and CIA, as well as the Agency, she had all the equipment a well-stocked gemologist would and more. She sat down on a metal stool in front of a microscope, slipped on a pair of plastic gloves and held out her palm. Gabriel gave her the bracelet in a plastic bag.

She removed the piece of jewelry and placed it on the stage of the scope, then adjusted the lenses using a large black knob at the base on the unit. Gabriel waited.

She continued to peer through the eyepieces, her voice muffled. "You want this hair, I assume?"

"Yes."

Without looking, she reached over and picked up a pair of tweezers from a pile of tools to her right. Carefully removing the single blond hair, she slipped it into another plastic bag and returned to her work. She turned the bracelet this way and that, then finally, a few minutes later, she looked up. Grabbing a book from the shelf above her table, she flipped through the pages until she found the right spot.

She jabbed her finger at the color photograph. "This is it," she said. "The stamp on the clasp."

Gabriel leaned over and studied the picture.

"It was made in Italy. Eighteen-karat gold. Nice work but not terribly expensive or creative. A factory piece, for sure."

"Factory?"

"It wasn't custom ordered," she explained. "The company probably made thousands like it. Be impossible to trace."

"But it came from Italy?"

"It was *made* in Italy," she corrected him. "A lot

of jewelry is manufactured there. The pieces are exported all over the world. This could have been purchased two blocks from here. Or two thousand miles away."

"Is it a man's bracelet or a woman's?"

She took out a gauge and measured the bracelet for length and width. "Seven and three-quarters...four millimeters wide." She made a sound, pursing her lips as she thought. "A typical woman's piece is seven inches, a man's bracelet, eight inches or longer. A large-boned woman or a small-boned man could wear it." She held up the piece and stared at it. "The design goes by several different names, but it's usually called San Marco. It's been around forever."

"Can you tell me more?"

"Sure—but it'll take time. I'll do all the standard tests then I'll contact the manufacturer and see what they can tell me. Typically that's not much, though. When do you need the information?"

"Yesterday?"

"Right. You and everyone else. Get in line."

"A woman's life depends on it."

"Someone's life *always* depends on it." She looked up then and saw his expression. Her own changed swiftly. "I'll do my best."

He put his hand on her shoulder and squeezed. "I appreciate the help, Marybeth."

"I know you do...the question is does *she* appreciate it, too?"

"Not now," he answered. "But she will in the future…if she has one."

He left the lab shortly after that, stopping two doors down to drop off the hair sample with one he'd taken from Alex's hairbrush. "I need a comparison," he told the tech. "Do whatever you have to—I just want to know if these came from the same person." The man nodded and promised to get right on it. Gabriel finished up at Evan Frank's office.

The lanky agent raised his head as Gabriel halted at the door. "Got anything for me?" he asked.

"Not yet. Villard's in some Podunk New Jersey village. It's gonna take the agent some time to get out there."

"Well, tell him to hurry."

"I did tell him." Frank leaned back in his chair and stared at Gabriel. "What is it about this one, man? The case is ten years old, for God's sake."

"Yeah, and somebody's been waiting all that time to make Alex Worthington dead. Whoever it is, is determined and motivated. I'd like to know a name before the worst happens."

"It's always been your bête noire, hasn't it?" Frank asked all at once. "This case and everything associated with it."

The agent's words made Gabriel remember Alex's question. *Why,* she'd asked. *Why do you even care…?*

Evan Frank's eyes were speculative when Gabriel didn't answer. "You can't let go of it, can you?"

"You've got it backward." Gabriel said, shaking his head slowly. "The *case* won't let go of *me*."

ALEX TURNED AWAY from Libby as quickly as she could. Libby was wrong, flat out wrong, but Alex couldn't explain enough to convince her. "I'm going to fix some coffee," she said, heading for the kitchen. "Would you like some, too?"

Libby followed Alex but stopped at the doorway. "No, thanks," she said. "I don't have much time."

Grateful she'd been able to divert the girl, Alex continued with her preparations, lifting cups and saucers from the cabinet, retrieving coffee beans from the refrigerator. "What's the hurry?"

"I've got an appointment with Dad's doctor," she said. "I want to talk to him about Dad."

Alex turned in alarm. "Why? Is he getting worse—"

"He's holding his own, but that's not good enough. I want more than that. I know there's got to be something else we can do. The doctor just isn't trying hard enough."

Pity swept over Alex. She put down the grinder and came to where Libby stood. "Honey...your dad... He's very sick. The doctor's doing everything he can."

"That's what Daddy said."

"So what are you trying to accomplish? You're only going to upset yourself."

The girl's eyes filled and she shook her head, a curtain of red hair falling about her face. "I don't know," she whispered. "I just feel like…like I ought to be doing something besides standing there and watching him die."

Alex took Libby's chin in her hand and lifted her face. "You're doing exactly what you're supposed to be doing," she said. "You're loving him. That's the only thing any of us can do right now."

"But it's not enough."

"I agree," Alex said. "It isn't. But it's all we've got. Everything else is outside our control."

Libby's face crumpled. Alex reached out and held her tightly, the young woman's sobs shaking her body. For what seemed like a long time, but was only a few minutes, she continued to cry. Alex grabbed a handful of tissues from a box on the counter and gave them to her.

"I'm sorry," Libby said brokenly. "It's…it's just so sad…"

"Yes, it is." Alex led her into the living room, abandoning the unmade coffee. They sat down on the sofa. "Your dad doesn't want us to be sad, though. So it doesn't help him when you are."

Libby nodded. "But it's hard not to be."

"I know." Alex let her eyes drift to the window. The blinds were still closed tight—Gabriel's doing—and her thoughts went to him and his words from the night before. "But we all have hard things we have to do, sweetheart."

"Not like this."

"You might be surprised."

Libby didn't seem to hear Alex. A strange mix of adult and teen, she sat quietly, her thoughts on herself. Finally, as if coming out of a trance, she looked at Alex. "You are still coming for Christmas, aren't you?"

Oh, God... In the wake of all the craziness, Alex had completely forgotten her promise. She hesitated. "With Gabriel here, it might be difficult..."

"Oh, Alex, you've got to come. I—I don't think I can do it by myself." Libby dabbed at her eyes with a wadded tissue. "Can't you bring him with you?"

Libby's revelation about Ben still loving her echoed in Alex's mind. She'd suspected for a long time he still had feelings for her. "I don't think your dad would appreciate me bringing company."

Libby's expression shifted again, from uncertain youth to adult maturity. "I disagree," she said. "In fact, I think he'd like it."

Alex tilted her head in surprise. "Why?"

"You said it yourself—he wants us to be happy. If he knows you're in love again and you have someone in your life, he'd be glad. That way he won't feel like he's abandoning you when he..." Her voice trailed off and got thick. "When he...you know..."

Libby's analysis rocked Alex. The details of the

kiss and the look and the touch had all been recorded in the twenty-year-old's romantic mind. Ben would hear everything and then some. If Alex didn't show up, Ben would think she'd deserted him before he could desert her...

She and Gabriel would have to go, if only for a little while.

"All right," she finally said. "We'll be there."

GABRIEL LOCKED his car, then made his way across the parking lot and up the stairs to Alex's unit. He'd wanted to return before Libby left, but he'd stayed longer than he'd planned, forcing Evan to call New Jersey a thousand times. It'd been a pointless exercise. The agents there would move on it when they could, which wasn't today. Alex opened the door as soon as he tapped on it.

She looked distressed, her eyes darker than usual, a smudge of blue smeared on one high cheekbone. He reached out and rubbed the spot. "Paint," he explained. Her skin felt like glass, smooth and cold.

She barely seemed to notice. "We have to go to Ben's on Christmas," she said without preamble. "I promised him I'd be there, but I'd forgotten."

Gabriel shrugged from his coat and draped it over the couch. "That's fine," he said.

Without another word, she went to the kitchen and he followed. She made a distracted gesture toward the counter where she'd been making a late lunch. "Would you like something to eat?"

He started to answer but she didn't wait to hear what he said. She grabbed two pieces of bread, her movements quick and jerky. Gabriel immediately turned suspicious. Had something happened? He walked over and put his hand on hers, stopping her as she slathered mustard over a slice of bread.

When their eyes connected, Gabriel thought of Toni, the woman in San Diego, the one who'd moved in and out of his life so quickly. Something dark and hidden had flickered in Alex's gaze, immediately reminding him of the other woman. A second later he realized what it was. Both of them hid a deep vulnerability that had somehow become integral to their lives. They'd each been hurt and now the remnant of that pain was woven into their faces. The scars could have made them frail, or even bitter, but instead they'd both been left with a strength that surprised him. The eerie similarity disturbed him but he didn't stop to examine it. He was afraid he wouldn't like what it said about himself.

"What's wrong?" His eyes held hers.

She shook her head quickly. "Nothing. Nothing's wrong."

She started to return to her task but he wouldn't let her, his fingers tightening on her wrist. "You're lying to me," he said. "I can see you're upset."

She closed her eyes for just a second, then opened

them again. "It's getting to me," she said after a moment. "Nothing in my life is the same. You're here, I'm lying to Libby, someone's after me... I don't like any of it and it's making me nervous."

"What else?"

She made a sound of disbelief. "Isn't that enough? Most normal people would be a little upset right now, wouldn't they? A little worried?"

At some point—while she was talking, but he didn't know when—Gabriel's grip on her arm had turned into something else. He was stroking the inside of her wrist with the pad of his thumb. He could feel the ridge of her scar beneath her bracelet...and beneath the scar he could feel her pulse.

"Gabriel?"

"Yes," he answered automatically. "Any sane person would be worried. And scared and concerned and everything else. But you don't need to be."

"I don't need to—" She broke off in midsentence, skepticism filling her voice. "Forgive my ignorance but why do say that?"

"You've got me." He paused. "And I'm not going to leave until this is resolved."

He let his eyes go over her face, each plane and contour known to him. The unexpected connection should have shocked him, but it didn't. All it did was make him want her even more.

For Gabriel, the clock stopped ticking as she clearly read the intent in his eyes. But she didn't move. Instead, she waited as he did, both of them paralyzed by the shadowed past they shared and the uncertain future they faced. Gabriel told himself a better man would walk away and leave her alone, but he wasn't a better man.

He bent his head toward her and kissed her.

ALEX TASTED Gabriel's lips, the faint scent of his skin coming to her as she lifted her hand and touched his jaw. She could hear someone playing the television in the apartment next door but the sound came from a different world than the one she was in. Her world—her universe—had suddenly shrunk to one reality. She was in Gabriel's arms and he was kissing her. Not for the benefit of someone else, not because he wanted to put on a show. He was kissing her because he wanted to.

And she wanted it, too.

She flashed through an astonishing range of emotions as his mouth pressed hers and his tongue parted her lips. Other details registered through the fog. The compact muscularity of his body. The span of his hands against her back. Through the thin sweater she wore, she could feel his chest and shoulders.

He continued to kiss her, his lips tasting hers as he dropped feathery touches over her cheeks and neck, caressing her skin in the lightest possible way. She felt as if he'd picked up one of her paintbrushes and was sweeping it over her face. Her reaction was so strong she could hardly bear to face it...but she had to. Because she suddenly desired Gabriel with a need unlike any she'd ever felt.

She groaned with a guttural sound, an almost primeval acknowledgment of the urge building inside her. All at once, she wanted him to stop kissing her. She wanted him to pick her up and carry her down the hall to the lonely bedroom where she slept by herself. She wanted him to put her down on the wide, white bed and take off her clothing. She wanted him to make love to her until she forgot who she was and where she'd been.

As though reading her mind, he took her by the arms.

And then he pushed her away.

CHAPTER ELEVEN

DUMBFOUNDED AND SILENT, Alex stood before Gabriel, her mouth tender, her body trembling. She didn't know which was more painful—experiencing his kiss when she knew she shouldn't or feeling so alone when he stepped back and dropped his embrace.

Gabriel regarded her with his usual scrutiny, but behind his flat expression there was something that stopped Alex's heart. Was it regret? Was it desire? Was it pity? She couldn't define the emotion, but whatever it was, she wanted no part of it. Things were already too confusing.

With Libby's observation echoing in her mind, Alex turned away from Gabriel. After a moment had passed, she spoke carefully, her back still to him. "You're right," she said as if he'd asked an important question. "That shouldn't have happened."

When he didn't answer, she faced him once more. His gaze was focused on her with the intensity of a laser, but his voice was calm as ever. "We don't have to analyze it. Things happen. That's all." He shrugged, his wide shoulders moving under his jacket, the black leather rasping in the quiet.

He walked away from her and opened the refrigerator door. Taking out a cold bottle of water, he drank deeply then looked at her, his hand coming down slowly as their eyes met. His gaze flashed again and he started to cross the room toward her, but she stopped him with a shake of her head, her heart pounding harder than it should have. She didn't need him any closer. The kitchen seemed smaller than it had been moments before. She stepped around him and returned to her task. Gabriel remained silent until she picked up a cheese slicer and slab of cheddar.

"I got some info on the bracelet."

The words were meant to divert her and they did. Alex jerked her head up, her hands stilling.

"It was made in Italy," he said. "Eighteen karat. Pricey but not over the top." He took another draw from the bottle. "Too common to trace."

She nodded then finished the sandwiches, taking them to a small table beside the window, along with a cup of coffee. The ham and cheese tasted like ashes.

Gabriel took the chair opposite hers, but he didn't eat. He simply drank his water and regarded her. His steady stare made her nervous but she wouldn't give in and look at him. She chewed mechanically.

Finally he spoke. "Did Libby have bad news?"

Alex explained the young woman's anxiety over her father's health.

"He's not going to make it, is he?"

"No." She shook her head, relaxing a bit, the conversation once again impersonal. "Ben's dying. Libby knows that but she can't accept it. She's never lost anyone before. Her mother passed away giving birth to her. Ben's all she has."

"She's got you."

"We're close, that's true." She nodded, Gabriel's observation surprising her. "But I can't take Ben's place. He's her father and she loves him dearly."

"You were there when she was younger. It was hard, but you stuck with her. She looks at you as if you were her mother."

Alex dabbed at her mouth with her napkin then dropped it to the table, his words taking away the last of what little appetite she'd had.

"Exactly how long have you been following me?" she asked. "How long have you been in my life without my knowledge?"

He realized he'd given himself away. Libby had had her problems during her early teens, just like most kids. Fourteen, fifteen...those had been the worst. Alex had been on shaky ground herself, still struggling yet trying to make her new marriage successful. She'd wondered if she could cope with the rebellious girl.

He shrugged. "A while."

"How long is 'a while'?"

He took another swallow then looked at her straight on. "Since the beginning."

"Since the beginning? You mean—"

"As soon as I...finished things up, I came to Texas."

His statement struck her hard, like a fist against her breastbone. He'd been here all along, seen her bad times, watched her disintegrate? She started to question him then something else registered. "What does that mean?" she asked. "How did you 'finish things up'?"

His answer was a stare.

"Don't do that to me," she said tightly.

"Don't ask questions I can't answer."

Taking a deep breath, she forced herself to look out the window. He'd kept an eye on her for years, watching and waiting. The knowledge that he'd been there—throughout everything—should have made her mad, *would* have made her mad a few weeks ago. Now, strangely enough, as she examined it closer, she had an entirely different reaction. But she didn't welcome this one any more than she would have the anger. Truth be told, she'd have been more comfortable with the anger than what she was feeling.

She took a sip of her coffee then put the cup down. "Why didn't you let me know you were around? Why didn't you tell me?"

"You wouldn't have wanted to know," he said,

his voice flat. "And you wouldn't have wanted me here."

His tone tipped her off. As always with Gabriel, there was more to the situation than he had revealed.

"And?" she said. "There's another reason, too, isn't there?"

"I had to be careful." He waited a second. "Extremely careful. I couldn't take the risk of contacting you even if I'd wanted to."

"Why not? What difference would that have made?"

His eyes flicked to the window beside them then back to her. "My goal was to protect you, Alex, not lead the killers to you.

"I wasn't sure it was safe, but you were doing okay," he continued. "You didn't need me complicating the situation."

"If you thought I was doing 'okay,' I'd hate to know what you define as 'not okay.'"

"I knew you'd survive."

"Then you knew more than I did."

"You're a strong woman, Alex. You'd been through hell and back but that didn't change who you are." He tapped his chest. "Inside here. You have a different name and a different life, but *you're* the same person."

"I was a kid. Everything familiar to me was taken away in one fell swoop." Her voice grew heated.

"My family, my life, my sense of security—I didn't know who in the hell I was, how could you?"

"I knew," he said with conviction. "And I also knew you'd be okay—eventually. The only time I got concerned was when you married."

"You were worried about Ben?" Surprise rippled over her. "He's a good man. You shouldn't have been concerned."

"He may be the best man in the world but he wasn't the one *you* needed."

She flared. "How did you know that?"

"The same way I knew you'd survive—I knew you," he replied. "And I knew you were looking for something that he wasn't going to give you."

"Which was?"

"Your old life." He picked up his sandwich. Then he put it back down without tasting it.

Alex wanted to argue the point, but she couldn't, because Gabriel was right. Ben had been older and wiser, wealthy and stable. She'd thought he could protect her, thought that he could make everything okay again and make her feel safe once more. She'd been wrong.

"I had to try," she said softly.

"I know," he said. "That's why I didn't stop you."

They stared at each other through a patch of watery sunlight. His face was etched with weariness but it wasn't the kind that sleep could erase. He'd been worn down by his past. The past they shared…and the responsibilities it had brought to him. He had his own nightmares, and like hers, they didn't disappear when dawn broke.

The sudden realization sent her spinning. She'd never stopped to wonder what had happened to him after New Mexico. In the years that had passed, he'd been in her mind, of course, but only in the context of fear. She'd never considered what the situation had meant to him, done to him. She'd only seen it through the filter of her *own* pain, nothing else.

She'd lost her world and blamed him for it. In return, he'd kept her safe.

As she understood what that meant, the links that bound them shifted and grew tighter. Alex felt herself drawn to Gabriel, her heart tumbling into a place it had never been before. Unable to stop the fall, she was powerless against the strength of her attraction.

But fright followed, and the two intertwined like vines grown together.

Alarm and desire. Danger and safety. Peril and refuge. Which was which?

GABRIEL HAD FACED foreign assassins, natural disasters and countless other difficulties. None of them could compare to the challenge of living with Alex and not touching her.

He'd known the minute he'd kissed her—hell, he'd known the minute *before*—that he was taking them down a path they should avoid, but he hadn't stopped himself until it was too late. He'd avoided entanglements like this all his life—had shied away from them completely—and now he knew why. Failure had a price he couldn't afford. If he wasn't vigilant, if he didn't keep him mind on his work, they could both end up dead.

Following Alex down the aisle of the grocery store late one afternoon a few days later, Gabriel marveled at the seeming normalcy of what they were doing. All around them people were chattering and shopping, buying what they needed for their upcoming holiday meals. It felt bizarre to be in the store, pushing a metal cart and filling it with boxes and cans. Countless other men were doing the same, trailing behind wives or girlfriends, but the bored looks on their faces were a direct contrast to his own. Every nerve ending he had was charged, each trying to be the first to scream danger.

Angling the cart around a crowded corner, he replayed the morning phone call he'd gotten from Evan Frank. The news the agent had given Gabriel should have made him happy, but it'd left him more unsettled than ever.

"Our man finally went to New Jersey," Frank had reported.

"And?"

"And your guy wasn't there."

Gabriel's curse had filled the telephone line. "Dammit to hell, Frank. Are you sure?"

The gangly agent chuckled. "Oh, yeah. I'm sure all right. He wasn't there because he's dead. Vail Villard was murdered a few weeks ago trying to buy drugs. He flashed a roll on a neighborhood corner and ended up getting more than he bargained for."

"You're sure it was a bad drug deal?"

"Positive. The local P.D. has already arrested their bad guy. He had Villard's stash and the keys to his car. To top it off, he confessed."

Gabriel asked more questions, but by the time he'd finished, he knew Villard couldn't have been the one behind Alex's problems. Not unless the man could teleport himself. Disgusted, he'd hung up without even thanking Frank. All they had now was the bracelet, which was damn little. Marybeth had called him even earlier that morning with her own dead end. And as he'd suspected all along, the blond hair caught on the clasp had been Alex's.

Frustration, cold and hard, formed a knot in Gabriel's chest. What was he supposed to do with so little information?

Alex finished her shopping and led him to the front of the store. They checked out quickly despite the crowd, and a few minutes later they were in Gabriel's car, heading for the apartment. She'd had to have groceries, she'd told him some time after lunch, but glancing across the Toyota's battered seats now, Ga-

briel suspected she'd needed diversion more than
bread.

He hadn't prevented her from going anywhere, but
her time outside the apartment had been minimal
since the drowning attempt. When she did leave, he'd
followed, although she hadn't known it. Mostly she
went into the bedroom where she worked and painted,
hour after hour. On occasion the phone would ring
and she would chat, but the conversations were always short, any invitations turned down, albeit gra-
ciously. He sensed this solitary life hadn't just started,
either. Alex was a loner. The minute her family had
been taken from her, her trust in people had disappeared as well.

Over the past few days, though, her nervousness
had grown. Strung between him and whoever wanted
to kill her, she was even more anxious than when
she'd first called him. When he'd told her about Villard, she'd listened closely, her head tilted to one side,
her stare focused on him. She'd reminded him of a
cat, sleek and edgy, ready to run. The idea of her
slipping away, in the dark, unnoticed and unprotected,
was one he couldn't contemplate.

Stopping at the next light, he looked at her again.
Her skin was drawn tight and she was worrying the
necklace that hung around her slender throat. Her face
looked haunted. He made up his mind quickly and
wheeled the car to the right.

''This isn't the way home,'' she said.

"I know that. We're not going back to the apartment. It's time we took a break," he declared.

"But the groceries—"

"The groceries can wait. We need some time off."

ALEX TENSED as Gabriel got on the MoPac freeway and headed north. Within minutes she knew where he was going, and a little bit later, he proved her right. Swinging the Toyota into the small lot beside Fonda San Miguel, he parked then switched off the engine. Without saying a word, he climbed from the car and came to her side, opening the door and putting out his hand. "Come on...I promised you a meal here."

Alex hesitated. She didn't want to go into the restaurant and sit across the table from Gabriel. She didn't want to make small talk or share dinner or laugh over a silly joke. They didn't have that kind of relationship and they never would. She looked up at him and began to say so, but he read her mind. Reaching down, he took her hand in his and pulled her out of the vehicle. A moment later they were standing in the darkened, plant-filled foyer, a nearby fountain gurgling peacefully, the cry of a caged parrot adding his call to the water's sound.

The dining room was virtually empty. The lunchtime crowd had come and gone and it was still early for dinner. A few people sat at the bar lining the back wall, but their voices were muted. A black-garbed waiter finally noticed Gabriel and Alex and took them to the front of the restaurant, to a spot by the window.

"Can we have that one instead?" Gabriel nodded toward a smaller table in the corner of the room.

The waiter murmured his consent, and Alex followed the two men in silence. Now that her eyes had been opened, she saw everything Gabriel did through a different framework. As she took the chair the waiter pulled out, she glanced back at the table Gabriel had rejected. It faced a busy street, traffic—by foot and by car—sped by only a few yards away. A quick shot and an easy escape. Did that kind of assessment come naturally to Gabriel? Had he always been that way?

She knew nothing of how he'd become the man he was. And he knew her darkest secrets.

It seemed strange to be so ignorant of his past. The first thing she usually did with most people was ask them about their families, their history, their past. Over the years she'd developed this technique because once people started talking about themselves they would forget to ask her questions. On a deeper level, hearing the stories filled a void in Alex's psyche. She *needed* to know their histories. Maybe because he was the only person who really knew her, Alex hadn't felt the same way about Gabriel. But she did now. Suddenly she wanted to know everything about him, but she had no idea how to ask.

They ordered something to drink and when the

waiter came back a few minutes later, they sipped in silence, Alex unable to throw off her sudden awkwardness. The huge but empty dining room was strangely intimate. After a bit her courage grew. She spoke quickly, before she could change her mind.

"Tell me who you are."

He understood the question immediately. She could tell by the wariness that came into his eyes.

"There's not much to tell." His accent deepened, she noticed, when he wasn't watching himself. The up-and-down cadence, so different from her own, was strong now.

"Then it won't take long." She smiled slightly, then turned serious. "I need to know."

He nodded. But he didn't say anything.

"Where are you from?" she prompted him. "You didn't grow up here, in the States."

"I spent my childhood in Dublin."

Each word was spoken with reluctance, each fact given up with reservation. Was it habit or something darker?

"Brothers?" she pressed. "Sisters? Crazy aunts and uncles?"

"Plenty of the latter," he said. "No sisters. Four brothers, all younger."

"Where do they live? Are you close to them?"

"They're here and there. London. New York. One's still in Dublin. One's in Cairo."

"You don't see them often?"

"No."

"What about your mom and dad?"

"My da is dead."

"I'm sorry...tell me about him. What did he do?"

"He worked for An Garda Síochána."

She butchered the words but repeated what he'd said. "An Garda Síochána?"

"Ireland's national police," he explained. "He was a cop."

Things fell into place, and Alex nodded, repeating the exotic term.

"It means Guardians of the Peace. They don't carry weapons, just wooden truncheons."

He smiled in an ironic way then sipped his drink. When he set the tumbler down, he did so precisely, as if it mattered that he got it just right. "Peace was the last thing we had in our house, though. My da thought the evening wasn't complete if he didn't beat the crap out of one of us boys."

The pain in his voice was so deep and ingrained that Alex felt it instantly, a sympathy she didn't want swelling inside her. "Where was your mother? Couldn't she stop him?"

"My mother was the reason he beat us. She disappeared when I was seven." He turned the glass slowly, the scotch inside catching light and turning it into gold. He lifted his eyes and they glittered like the drink. "He couldn't beat her for escaping so he had to make do with us."

Once again, Alex's heart ached—first for the woman who'd suffered so much she'd had to flee her children, and then for the children she'd left behind, abandoned and empty. Gabriel had had no one but himself to depend upon, even as a youngster. His character had been forged by his own perseverance. "Do you ever hear from her?"

"She disappeared," he repeated. "No one ever saw or heard from her."

"Ever?" She looked at him in amazement.

"Ever." The word held more finality than usual. "I still wonder sometimes if he killed her...but the chances are greater that she killed herself."

Alex froze, the weight of her gold bracelets suddenly heavier than they'd been a second before, the weight of *everything* suddenly heavier. She frequently told herself she wasn't the only one who'd ever lost her family, but Gabriel's revelation shocked her deeply. Every time she'd accused him of not understanding... The circumstances were different, of course, but that didn't matter. At least she'd had her childhood. He'd missed his completely.

"I—I'm sorry," she stuttered, not knowing what else to say.

"It happened too long ago to be sorry for it now." He threaded a hand through his thick black hair as if to dislodge the memories. "I survived."

"Life is about more than just surviving."

"Is it?" He lifted his glass and drained it, holding two fingers up to the waiter to order another round.

"Of course it is," she answered sharply. "You don't just go through the motions. What point is there in that?"

"Sometimes that's all you have."

"I know," she said. "Believe me, I *know*. But if you're here and living, then it needs to be more than that."

GABRIEL STARED at Alex through the gloom. Her vehemence surprised him. But instead of saying so, he reached across the white linen tablecloth and took her arm. Turning it over, he traced the scar under her bracelet with his thumb. He could barely feel it, but he knew it was there.

"You haven't always felt that way," he said, looking into her eyes.

"No, I haven't. But killing yourself isn't about life. It's about control."

He felt her pulse coursing beneath his thumb. "Control?"

She nodded. "Maybe your mother understood that."

"Well, I don't."

"That's because you've never lost it," she said quietly. "As an adult, you've always been in charge of your life, in command of what's going on around you. As soon as you reached adulthood, you made sure of that. Since then, you've never had someone else tell you how and where and why you're going to live.''

Her words surprised him, although he tried not to show it. "I always thought suicide was about escape."

"Only in the sense that you're escaping from whatever has dominance over you. And that could be anything from another person to your own mind." She looked down, her eyes focusing on his fingers. "I was in control of nothing." Her voice was so soft he could barely hear it. "My life was gone. I'd lost my family, my history, my name... I desperately wanted to regain power." She lifted her gaze. "At the time, I thought it was the only option, but now..."

"But now?"

"Now I know it's not an answer, period. There's always a way you can recapture your life, reclaim what you lost. You just have to find it."

The intensity of her words triggered something inside Gabriel, and suddenly he understood why she'd called him. Her life, such as it was, had finally been in her hands. Her job, her friends, her home—she'd arranged it as she'd wanted. Then—once again—someone had violated that order by breaking into her house and taking the one thing she cared about, her drawing. The loss of control must have been terrifying...because she knew how hard it would be to get it back. Before, when she'd been younger, she'd had no idea of what was ahead of her. This time she'd known and it'd scared her so much she'd called him, in spite of herself.

Thank God.

Behind Gabriel, the waiter cleared his throat. Taking the menus he offered, they studied the list then Alex ordered for them both.

When the man left the table, Gabriel realized he'd never released Alex's wrist. Her skin was warm and soft and he was caressing it slowly, dragging his thumb up and down the soft side of her arm. In the dim light, he lifted his gaze and their eyes connected, the communication between them silent but instantly understood.

When the morning light broke, they'd be in each other's arms.

CHAPTER TWELVE

ALEX ATE SPARINGLY. The food was as wonderful as always but she tasted nothing, her stomach nervous and tied up with stress. Mainly she drank her iced tea and watched Gabriel. It seemed amazing he looked the same as always because, to her, he had become a different man over the past few weeks. Which was one of the reasons she hadn't wanted to come here and eat with him. She was seeing him as someone else, someone new...someone intriguing. And now he'd managed to do what no man had ever done before. He'd made her explain herself.

She'd almost managed to convince her brain this meant nothing, when his eyes captured hers. A deep, gut-wrenching longing came over her to share even more, to let him into her life in a way she had never allowed anyone, including Ben. She'd didn't want to even think about the absurdity of it, but all at once she wondered if she was falling in love with Gabriel O'Rourke.

The idea was so impossible she immediately dismissed it. When Gabriel spoke a second later, she was grateful for the distraction.

"Do you enjoy your work?" he asked.

She felt her shoulders ease—a neutral topic. "Yes and no. When I get a student who's really creative, who's really artistic, it's a miracle to see his talent grow. All I have to do is harness some of the energy and get it moving in the right direction. Then I stand back and watch."

"And the others?"

"The others are tougher. I have to dig deeper to find their ability. Sometimes I need a really big shovel." She marveled at how calm she sounded, how ordinary the moment appeared to be.

"They're lucky to have you. Your paintings are incredible."

She raised her hand to her necklace, suddenly unsure at the thought of Gabriel knowing her work. "You've seen my work?"

"I've visited a few of the galleries that carry your paintings, yes..." He arched one dark eyebrow. "I'm surprised that you teach. You could make a very good living simply painting, I would think."

"The art world is fickle. I could become unpopular at any moment and I wouldn't be able to give the canvases away." She frowned. "It's not a dependable way to earn a paycheck."

"And you like things you can depend on?"

"Absolutely."

He nodded as if he'd known what her answer would be. They talked a bit more, then Gabriel signaled for the check, the situation seemingly relaxed. Underneath the veneer, however, Alex couldn't ignore the tension that was building.

He hadn't touched her once since he'd released her wrist, but he didn't need to. She felt each stare, each look, each word as if he were reaching across the table and caressing her gently. She trembled under the sensation, growing warmer and warmer. As soon as the waiter presented the bill, Gabriel opened the leather folder then slipped some cash inside. He looked over at her and waited, his hands motionless on the table. His gaze burned into hers. "Are you ready?"

Was she imagining things or did his words have a double meaning?

Not waiting for her answer, Gabriel stood and held his hand out. She took it and rose from the table. The ride home took forever but it was over in an instant.

GABRIEL UNLOCKED the door and stepped inside the now-dim apartment, pulling Alex in behind him. As always, he kept his body in front of hers, but this time, more than ever, he had a hard time concentrating. Against his back, he could feel the warmth of her curves, of her softness...of her desire.

Or was it his own?

He focused his concentration, waited and listened.

Everything seemed fine but he would check the rooms as he did each time they returned. "Wait here," he said over his shoulder.

When he came back a few minutes later, Alex was exactly where he'd left her—leaning against the front door. Her eyes were closed. He tried to imagine what she was thinking, but he couldn't. All he could hear were his own startling thoughts.

I want her more than I've wanted any other woman. And I always have...

Obviously sensing his presence, she opened her eyes slowly. He came closer until they were near enough to touch—he could see her pulse at the bottom of her throat and a gleam of gold, could smell her shampoo and her soap—but he didn't reach for her. He wasn't sure why, but it seemed monumentally important that she make the first move, and he made a vow that nothing would happen unless she initiated it.

A heartbeat passed. And then another. Gabriel had enough time to regret his vow.

Then she lifted her hands and put them on either side of his jaw. His heart jolted but he remained motionless while she molded her touch over the contours of his face. She had strong fingers with short, tapered nails. Moving them over his cheeks and then upward to his forehead, she explored the shape of his bones and the planes of his features. Finally, he remembered the potter's wheel in the workroom, the paintbrushes, the other tools of her trade. She was an artist. She saw with her touch as much as with her eyes.

She stopped, her palms resting lightly where she'd begun—against his jaw. Her hands had been cool but now they were warm. She'd taken on his heat and made it her own.

Gabriel reached up and took her hands. He turned them over and kissed the tender palms, then he looked at her, hesitating once again. He had to know if she was sure, if she knew what she was doing and what it meant. If she knew where this was taking them.

She shook her head before he could ask the question.

"Don't," she whispered. "Don't say a word. Pick me up and carry me to the bedroom."

She was setting the parameters. She wanted the release of sex, needed the warmth of another body, but that was all. She didn't want him to love her. She didn't want him to get too close. She didn't want what he wanted—but knew he'd never have.

A fleeting regret came and went but Gabriel didn't stop. He was who he was.

He lifted Alex into his arms and headed for the bedroom.

ALEX KNEW she was making the biggest mistake of her life. She'd pay dearly for this single moment of madness.

But she didn't care.

The only thing that mattered was how quickly Gabriel could satisfy the horrible longing that had made itself a home inside her heart. She'd had the need for such a long time it had become a part of her, but with Gabriel's arrival, the hunger had changed dimensions and now it was something else entirely, something over which she had no control.

He carried her easily, moving through the darkened apartment and heading for the bedroom. She blanked her mind to everything but the feel of his embrace.

He stopped beside the bed and Alex slid from his arms. Bending his head, Gabriel began to kiss her softly, his fingers behind her neck, warming her skin. A few minutes later, he unbuttoned the sweater she wore and slipped his hands inside.

It was a simple touch—his hands against her body—but her reaction was instantaneous. His palms seemed to sear her bare skin, a direct contrast to what she'd always thought of as his cold demeanor. The kiss they'd shared had given her a hint, and he'd touched her in the past, of course, but nothing like this.

She melted against him with a murmur and he responded accordingly. Tugging her sweater off her shoulders, he unfastened her bra and let it fall to the floor. For a frozen moment, he held her breasts, his thumbs easing over her nipples with the softest of caresses. She felt a corresponding thrill deep inside her. Then he dropped to his knees and pressed his face against her. A scent rose between them and she breathed it deeply, recognizing for the first time that it was the smell of him, of who he was. It was clean and sharp.

She reached down and pulled his sweater over his head. With her hands on his shoulders, he stayed where he was, nuzzling her breasts and kissing them. When he finally stood, she swayed, the power of his mouth and hands and touch making her dizzy.

He steadied her quickly, then took off the rest of his clothing. The clink of his belt buckle, the sound of the zipper that followed, the rustle of his pants—they were all sounds that would haunt her bedroom in the empty nights to come. But even that bittersweet realization wasn't enough to stop her. She wanted him too badly. She stared at him instead and burned the image of his naked body into her brain.

Through the slanted blinds, lines of light striped his form like strange tribal tattoos. He was much more muscular than she'd ever thought, his clothing as much a part of his camouflage as everything else. Now revealed, she could see the truth; a striking pair of shoulders and a wide chest, narrow hips and a rugged torso, arms and legs toned in the way of a man who'd kept himself in shape, not because he was vain, but because his life depended on it. He had scars, too. Not straight, perfect lines like the ones on her wrists but jagged reminders left by violence.

They came together in the center of the bed—tentatively at first, then greedily. All at once his hands were everywhere, his mouth following. Alex felt herself drowning in his touch, her breath stalling, her heart tumbling. This, she thought fleetingly, was what she'd been searching for over the years. She tried to label the sensation but it had no name, and a moment later, no importance either. She gave herself over to the desire that coursed through her blood.

GABRIEL'S HEART FOUGHT inside his chest. He'd been tied to Alex for the past ten years and now they would be connected in another, even deeper way. It was foolish to remind himself of the facts when they mattered least, but he almost felt an obligation to inject some reality. He failed miserably. The only truths he could recognize right now were those of the flesh— the satin of Alex's hair, the smell of her body, the taste of her skin. He lost himself, taking his time and focusing on the treasure of each. She moaned as his fingers and lips found sensitive places. Then—when she reached her limit—she pulled away from him, pushing his hands to the side so she could pay him back.

As she had touched his face, she now explored his body. Slowly and deliberately, each limb and every line, a separate thing to learn. He had the feeling she was storing the sensations inside her mind for later examination, but the idea of that didn't bother him. He was too busy doing the same.

After a while her touch became more insistent. Fueled by her passion, Gabriel rolled her over and held her arms above her head, her body stretched out beneath him. In the dim light, her eyes flared and that's when he knew her need was as great as his. Releasing her hands, he entered her with a groan.

They disappeared into a world of their own, one made real by their past but nonexistent in their future. Gabriel closed his eyes and wished he could stay forever.

ALEX WOKE UP abruptly. She'd been lost in a sleep so heavy it felt drug-induced, but something had brought her out of it. Her heart was pounding and every muscle in her body was tense. She was poised to flee and she had no idea why.

She glanced to the other side of the bed. Gabriel's still form lay motionless under the blankets, the rise and fall of his chest his only movement.

She held her breath and listened. Something had disturbed her—what was it?

She thought of waking Gabriel and put her hand out in his direction. Before she could touch him, though, she pulled her fingers back. She didn't need to depend on him and she shouldn't. They'd made love, yes, and a stronger link had been forged between them. But in the long run, did that matter? She had no illusions about what they'd done. There would be no picket fences, no tricycles, no happy endings in a future they shared. What had happened between them had not been rooted in a deep and abiding love. It'd simply been a release…because it *couldn't* be anything more.

Easing the covers away from her body, Alex swung her legs in slow motion to the side of the bed and reached for her robe. As she slipped it on, the faint sound of scratching broke the quiet. She froze in mid-movement, her pulse leaping into an irrational rhythm. Myriad possibilities flashed through her mind—she'd heard the neighbor's dog, a returning tenant, a mouse, for goodness' sakes! Just because she'd come awake frightened didn't mean she was in danger.

But then she heard the sound again. And this time she knew what it was. Someone was trying the lock to her front door.

Adrenaline shot into her bloodstream and fueled her into action. She was halfway to the bedroom door when she was grabbed from behind.

She would have screamed but his hand was over her mouth.

"What in the hell are you doing?" Gabriel growled, his voice a whisper.

With a toss of her head, she shook his fingers away from her lips. "There's someone breaking in," she whispered urgently. "At the front door." She tried to pull away from him but he held her fast.

"I know that." His eyes were cold and flat.

Her mouth fell open. "You know?"

"Get back in bed." He tilted his head toward the rumpled sheets. "I'll take care of this."

The temptation to follow his order was strong. But she couldn't. It'd be too easy to get used to that, to become accustomed to letting Gabriel take care of her. "No." She shook her head. "I've got to go see—"

The sound grew more insistent, halting Alex's protest as she threw a worried look toward the front of the apartment. Gabriel immediately took advantage of the moment. Dropping her arm, he grabbed a shirt, pulled it on and slipped past her. That's when she realized he already had on his jeans. And that's when she saw the gun in his hand. Dressed and ready, he'd been holding the weapon at his side all along—had probably had it in the bed as he feigned sleep. She shivered…and then she followed him.

He was behind the front door when Alex caught up with him. A look of fury crossed his face and he jerked his thumb toward the back, elbowing her away. She shook her head and resisted, reaching instead for her baseball bat.

Her fingers brushed the wood but she couldn't grasp the handle. The bat tottered in slow motion then crashed to the tiled entry.

Gabriel cursed and pushed Alex behind him, jerking the door open and bringing his gun up at the same

time. Alex stumbled backward with a cry then caught
her balance and followed him.

But she wasn't fast enough. By the time she had
reached the outside stairs, Gabriel had disappeared
into the darkness. She searched the parking lot with
frantic eyes, her heart pounding painfully against her
ribs. All she could see was one shadow chasing another...and then she heard gunfire.

CHAPTER THIRTEEN

THROWING HIMSELF between an SUV and a red Porsche, Gabriel cursed and glanced behind him. A round hole decorated the fender of the sports car exactly where his head had been a second before. The car's alarm began to blare as Gabriel ducked around the hood of the SUV, his weapon before him.

But the figure in black was nowhere to be seen. Dashing to the next vehicle, Gabriel studied the parking lot. He hadn't gotten a very good look as he'd tripped down the stairs, but he'd seen enough to confuse him. The gold bracelet popped in then out of his mind.

He made his way around the fence that surrounded the apartment complex, his eyes and ears alert. Fifteen minutes later, by the time he completed the circle and returned to where he'd started, the apartment's rent-a-cop was standing by the Porsche, his golf-cart commando unit parked to one side. Close by, an angry fat guy with a ponytail was screaming and sticking his finger in the hole on the fender. They both saw Gabriel at the same time.

He nodded at them in an affable way, the pistol tucked into his pocket with his shirt tail hiding it. "Got a problem?"

The bellicose security guard started to answer, but the other man cut him off. "A problem? Shit, yeah, I've got a problem! Look at that!" He pointed to the fender. "Hellfire and damnation! Who would do something like that to such a beautiful car?"

Gabriel thought the guy was going to break into tears. "That's a real shame," he agreed.

"You live here?" The guard stared at Gabriel suspiciously. "I never seen you before."

That's right, Gabriel thought. *You haven't seen me. You didn't see me break into Alex's apartment or see me carry her inside. You didn't see the person trying to get her tonight, either.*

"I'm just here visiting some friends," he said pleasantly. Sticking out his hand, he spoke. "Jack Brown."

The guard ignored Gabriel's outstretched hand. "What unit you in?"

"Building three."

"Who in Building three?"

The guard's questions were tiresome. On any other night, he'd be asleep in the cart somewhere on the back parking lot. His fast response wasn't something Gabriel had counted on. He gave the man the name of Alex's downstairs neighbor.

Seemingly satisfied, the guard said, "You didn't

notice anybody suspicious out here this evening, did you?''

Gabriel shook his head. ''No, I'm afraid not. I only came outside because the wife and I had a fight. I left in a hurry.'' He tried to look sheepish, glancing down at his open shirt. ''It's too damn cold to be that mad, though. I'm going back with my tail between my legs…''

They bid him goodbye and he walked away, his friendly pretense evaporating as soon as he was out of their sight. There had been something familiar, something he recognized, in the running figure, but what? Bounding up the steps to where Alex waited, Gabriel felt his throat go tight. He wanted to be angry with her—she should have stayed in the bedroom—but he couldn't dredge up the emotion. Her eyes were huge and shadowed by fear, her face the same color as the long white robe she wore.

She reached out as he came to the landing, her hand grabbing him. ''Are you all right? My God, I heard the gunshot and—'' She broke off to stare at his arm. A narrow red line trickled down his skin.

''It's just a scratch. I must have brushed against something when I was running.'' He cupped his hand around her elbow and guided her back inside the apartment. When the door was closed and locked, she shocked him by stepping into his arms. He held her trembling body tight, his hand at her nape, his desire to protect her so strong it scared him. She finally pulled back and looked up at him.

"I—I'm sorry, Gabriel. God, I screwed up everything," she said. "I—I wanted to help, that's all. I was reaching for the bat, and my fingers—"

"You should have stayed in the bedroom, Alex. Next time I tell you to do something like that, do it."

She looked as if she wanted to argue, but instead, she nodded. "Did—did you see him?"

"I got a look, but not much of one." He paused to gather his thoughts, to try and decide how much to tell her, but Alex realized immediately what he was doing.

She gripped his forearms with both her hands, her nails digging into his skin. "Tell me," she insisted.

He raised his gaze to hers. "Our visitor was a good shot. Dressed in black. On the smallish side…" His words faded.

"And? What else?" She knew there was more. "Did you see his face?"

"No, I didn't." He took a breath. "But it wasn't a man, Alex. The person at your door was a woman."

SHE DIDN'T KNOW WHY, but Alex was stunned at Gabriel's revelation. She stepped back from him. "Are—are you sure?"

"I'm sure. No man has curves like that." He removed his weapon from his pocket and switched on the safety catch, placing the gun on the table. Peeling off his shirt, he crossed to the couch where he sat down heavily and began to dab at the cut on his arm.

Alex sat down beside him. "What did she look like?"

"I didn't get near enough to register any details, but something about her seemed familiar…"

He fell silent, then lifted his head. His eyes were even darker than usual, frustration in their depths. "Do you have any enemies that are women? Someone you know who doesn't like you or—"

"There's no one like that. I don't have any enemies…or truly close friends. There's no one."

"Give it some thought. You've felt like someone was following you for quite a while. It's got to be someone who knows your routine, who knows where you work out. You might surprise yourself with whose name will come up."

"I'll try." She stood up then looked down at him. "But whoever it is, we're not going to be able to figure it out tonight. It's late—let me clean up your arm then you can get some rest. It's the least I owe you…"

"That's not necessary. I can—"

"I know you 'can,' anything," she interrupted him. "But I *want* to. Please let me."

She pulled him up from the sofa and they went down the hall to the bathroom, where she took alcohol and bandages from the counter beneath the lavatory. Gabriel perched on the edge of the tub. Cleaning the scratch, she realized at once it was worse than she'd thought. Deep and long, the angry-looking gash probably needed stitches.

"This looks bad, Gabriel." Dabbing at the bloody mess, she pulled her bottom lip between her teeth and fought a flip of squeamishness. "When was the last time you got a tetanus shot?"

"I'm covered." He held out his other arm and pointed to a ragged scar. "I got one when I did this last year."

She ran her finger over the crooked red line, then continued her ministrations. "What happened?"

"I had a problem in Bangladesh."

His answer wasn't really an answer, yet she knew it was all she would get. "And this?" She touched a puckered half-moon halfway down his back. "Same thing?"

"No. That was a bullet in Baku."

Moved by the image of his nomadic—and dangerous—life, she bent over and kissed the edge of his shoulder where a small patch of white skin stood out. Her lips poised over the spot, she lifted her questioning eyes to his.

"My youngest brother," he answered with a smile. "Hit me with a hot poker from the fireplace. Nearly set the house on fire, too."

With that, he pulled her closer to him and buried his head against her chest. Weaving her hands into his thick, dark hair, she stayed as she was. He held her tightly for several minutes, then he lifted his face and pulled her toward him, closing the gap between them, his mouth covering hers, his anger a thing of the past.

She took his hand and led him to the bedroom. She kissed the rest of his scars and he kissed hers, the healing touch of his lips against her wrists so tender and understanding that she wept. They made love until dawn. Afterward, Gabriel fell into an exhausted sleep, but rest eluded Alex. She stared at the ceiling and wondered how it was all going to end.

For the first time since her life had started over, she felt loved. How could it get any worse?

ON THE AFTERNOON of Christmas Eve, Libby phoned. "You are coming tonight, aren't you?" As she spoke to Alex, she tried to make her voice light, but she couldn't hide her heartache.

"Of course we'll be there," Alex said. "Gabriel and I are looking forward to it." She paused. "How's Ben doing?"

"Not good." Libby sighed. "The doctor came by last night. He looked serious when he left."

"Did you talk to him?"

"Yes, but all he said was that Dad was doing as well as he could expect." Futility laced her words. "What does that mean, Alex? 'As well as he could expect'? He should have just kept quiet for all the help that was."

Alex knew her answer would be harsh no matter how gently she spoke. She tried to soften her words, anyway. "It means he may not last much longer, sweetie. I think you need to prepare yourself."

The pause on the other end grew, then Alex heard Libby's muffled tears.

"I'm sorry, Libby," she said. "But it's a truth we can't deny anymore. You should start thinking about the future and what it's going to hold. That's what your dad wants you to do."

"Well, *I* don't want to... It's too hard."

"I know," Alex said. "And I agree. But we don't have a choice in the matter."

Libby made a sound of distress and Alex waited in silence. Deep down, Libby had to know Alex was right—they'd discussed this before. But knowing and accepting were two different things. Libby sniffed again, then spoke, her voice more steady. "Can you come early?"

"We'll be there as soon as you want us."

"Come at six," she said. "We'll eat dinner then open our presents."

"Six, it is."

Alex hung up the phone then raised her eyes to where Gabriel sat at the dining table, the last of their luncheon dishes scattered about, the morning's newspaper in his hands. If he'd heard any part of Alex's conversation, he gave no indication.

She studied him in the weak winter light coming

through the window. Would he ever tell her the truth about her parents? Did she even care anymore?

The very idea that she might not took away her breath, shocking her. Of course she still cared! Why wouldn't she? Everything she was, everything she'd experienced…it all came down to that one night ten years ago. And Gabriel had the key.

But in his arms she'd felt a fulfillment she'd never before experienced. The blinding moment had come and gone too swiftly, yet it'd lasted long enough to make her realize that everything—including her need to know about her past—was changing.

He rattled the paper. "Was that Libby?"

"Yes, it was." Alex forced her other thoughts to the side. "I promised her we'd be there at six. For dinner and presents."

He came to her side and ran the back of his finger over her cheek. It was one of a thousand gentle ways he'd touched her in the past week, but she still shivered beneath the caress. Like a lot of other things, his tender lovemaking was the exact opposite of what she had expected. Pulling her into his arms, he looked down at her, his dark eyes unreadable as always.

"Would you rather stay home?" he asked. "If going to the Worthingtons' will upset you—"

"I have to go," she interrupted. "It's not something I can ignore."

He nodded slowly, then after a second, he asked,

"What about us? Can you ignore what's going on there?"

She wasn't prepared for his directness. Her answer reflected her surprise. "I wouldn't want to," she said automatically. "But even if I did, I probably couldn't. I've never been very good at make-believe."

He understood her hidden meaning. "I'm going to catch up with whoever is behind all this, Alex. I promise you that. You don't have to worry."

"I know."

He tucked a strand of hair behind her right ear. "And you have nothing to fear from me, either. You never have."

"I understand that, too."

"Then what is it? What are you afraid of?"

"I'm not afraid of anything."

His arms tightened around her and he started to say something but she stopped him. "I just wasn't prepared for what's happened between us. I—I don't know how I'm supposed to feel about it."

"There isn't a set response."

"I know, but I didn't call you so we could end up in bed. That was the last thing on my mind."

"I'm well aware of that. It's not why I came, either. But it happened. Let's leave it at that for now."

She looked into his eyes and heard the past whisper in her ear. How on earth had she ever looked at him and thought he was cold? Cruel? Heartless?

She nodded because she had no other option and

he lowered his mouth to meet hers, delivering a warm, long kiss that left her wishing they'd never left the bedroom.

When he lifted his head, he looked as if he felt the same way, but an even deeper need came into his eyes, determination accompanying it.

"I don't want to leave you, but I've got to go see Evan Frank," he said. "He might not be in tomorrow and I want to see if he's come up with anything about our midnight visitor."

She almost felt relieved. "Go ahead. I have plenty of work to keep me busy."

He regarded her with a measuring glance, then he nodded and kissed her again, hard and fast. Her heart was still pounding when he disappeared through the door.

GABRIEL STARTED the Toyota's engine but he didn't put the car in gear. From his vantage point across the street, he could see Alex's apartment, his breath turning into cold puffs of air inside the vehicle.

He tried to convince himself to go. Whoever had tried to break in had not come back, and if she wanted to, she certainly wouldn't show up during the day. And if something did happen, he was growing more sure that Alex could handle it. Every day she reminded him more and more of Selena. And every day he knew he was getting in deeper and deeper. He should have controlled himself better and stayed out of Alex's bed. When the time came for him to leave—and it would—the goodbyes would not be easy. He only hoped they both lived long enough to say them.

With that thought, Gabriel reached for his cell phone. Evan Frank answered on the first ring.

"Can you come to Alex's apartment?" Gabriel didn't bother to say hello. "I'm parked off Oxford Street in front of her complex. I want to talk to you but I don't want to leave her. I've got a bad feeling…"

"I'm in a meeting, for God's sake—"

Gabriel didn't let the agent finish. "We need to talk about what happened. Have you got anything new on the break-in? Have you—"

"I'll call you when I finish—"

"This can't wait, Frank. And I don't want to have this conversation over the phone. I need to pick your brain in person."

"You've picked it clean already. There's nothing left."

Gabriel didn't answer. He waited patiently then Evan finally spoke, just as Gabriel had known he would.

"All right. I'll be there in fifteen minutes," he said with a sigh. "How do you like your coffee?"

Gabriel told him, then ending the call, he glanced at his watch and closed his mind to the topic, blanking out the rest of his thoughts. It was a skill he'd developed over the years while sitting in rat holes from one end of the world to the other, waiting for a good guy or a bad.

Seventeen minutes later, Frank's unmarked car pulled into the spot behind Gabriel's Toyota. The agent tapped on his horn and held up two Starbucks cups. Gabriel slipped from his vehicle and into Frank's where the aroma of hot coffee greeted him.

Frank handed Gabriel a cup, tilting his giraffe neck and shaking his head. ''There's nothing new, O'Rourke. And I don't really see how I can help you.''

Gabriel felt his frustration rise. ''There's got to be something going on here that we aren't seeing…''

''Okay…let's start at the beginning. Are you sure it was a woman at the door?''

''Absolutely.'' Gabriel nodded. ''But the strangest part about it is that she seemed familiar to me even though I didn't see her face. There was something about her…'' He took another sip of coffee, then looked across the fake-leather seats. ''Who was involved in the Mission case besides Selena? Were there any other women?''

Evan's hard-drive-like mind clicked and whirled, then spit out the information. ''There were four female agents on the case. They worked on it at various times, both before and after you were involved.''

''Who were they?''

Frank rattled off the names but they meant nothing

to Gabriel. He'd always worked alone at the Agency, no partners, male or female. But he might have seen them at some time. That would have been enough to trigger his thinking.

"You know any of them?" Gabriel asked. "What kind of people were they? What did they look like?"

Frank described each woman in detail, down to her dress size. "They were all solid agents. In fact, they still are. One's stationed in Moscow, one's in Gaza, one's—"

Gabriel cut him off. "What about the bad guys? Did they have women with them?"

"Not as far as the op went."

"What about personally? Wives, girlfriends, mistresses? All three?"

"I don't know about Villard. But you know Guy had a wife and a daughter. René had a girlfriend." He paused. "Now that you mention it, Guy had a mistress, too."

"Do you know where they are now?"

"The woman who lived with René is in Omaha. She's a schoolteacher."

"And Guy's two?"

"The mistress disappeared. Riva, his wife, went back to France, with their child, Antoinette. She and the kid slipped through customs, either at one of the airports or possibly at the Spanish border, we're not sure."

"But she definitely lives overseas?"

"The last time I checked she did."

"Check again."

Frank nodded.

"And look into René's situation, too. Make sure his ex is still where she's supposed to be. And see if you can find the mistress."

"All right."

Gabriel looked through the blurry windshield to Alex's apartment. The window was fogged by the vapor clinging to it, everything beyond it out of focus and vague. Just like his thinking. He thought again about the woman who had tried to break in. Something teased him, something just out of reach, but what?

"You mentioned Selena Mission…" Frank tapped the side of the steering wheel. "Is there any possibility this could be her?"

Gabriel turned back to stare at the agent. "I don't know. The last time I saw her was when Robert died. She vanished after that." He drained his cup then crumpled it, allowing it to fall from his fingers. He ignored Frank's pained expression as the container hit the plastic mat. "Why would she want to terrorize her own daughter, though? That doesn't make sense."

Frank stared at him quizzically. "Nothing makes sense in our world, Gabriel. Have you been out of touch so long you've forgotten that?"

Gabriel started to say no, then he stopped himself. His questions weren't a matter of remembering or not, because his judgment on the case had never been impartial. From the minute he'd walked inside the Mission home ten years ago and found Alexis, it'd been more than just another op to him. And now he was in even deeper. He couldn't answer Frank's question. All he did was shake his head.

CHAPTER FOURTEEN

DARK CAME EARLY that evening. Grateful for the time she'd had alone, Alex had finally managed to regain some of her emotional stability, but she wasn't sure how long her newfound balance would stay in place once she saw Gabriel.

He stood by the window in a dark double-breasted suit. With his hair freshly trimmed and his shave close, he looked sophisticated and refined. No one would ever suspect he'd lived the life he had. The sight of him sent her heart into a rhythm as rapid and out of control as the rest of her life.

Taking a deep breath, she entered the room. She had on one of Ben's favorites, her burgundy tuxedo-style pantsuit with satin lapels. Gabriel appraised her with a slow glance and she knew immediately—although it would go unsaid—that he liked the outfit as much as Ben. By the time he finished looking at her, she felt weak.

She touched her necklace, scared he might sweep her back into the bedroom, while secretly wishing he would. "Are you ready?"

He nodded, and twenty minutes later they parked outside Ben's lavish home. Gabriel cut the car's engine and whistled beneath his breath.

Alex followed his gaze. The house was huge and elaborate, a typical Austin mansion. Ben had had it built right after they'd married, thinking Alex would enjoy the luxurious surroundings. When it failed to mean anything to her, she'd sensed his disappointment. Material things had never impressed her. She'd wanted a home, yes, but to her, home meant something much different. Home meant family.

"That's some place," Gabriel said. "It must have been hard for you to give up after the divorce."

"Not really."

She didn't explain, but with Gabriel she didn't need to. Better than anyone she'd ever known, he understood what she left unspoken, an ability that also made her uneasy.

With a brisk wind whistling around them, they made their way up the sidewalk, packages filling their arms. Margaret opened the door while the bell was still pealing. "C'mon in, you two," she said cheerfully. "It's getting cold. You don't need to be standing out there."

Alex kissed Margaret's cheek, the smell of roasting turkey and sweet potatoes clinging to her skin. Turning to Gabriel, she introduced him to the smiling housekeeper, who took their coats and helped with their gifts.

Gabriel charmed Margaret exactly as Alex expected. Within moments, the older woman was leading him back to her kitchen, a deep discussion taking place between them on different dressing recipes. They reached the swinging doors before Margaret seemed to remember Alex. She turned and waved a hand toward the rear of the house. "Oh, honey, I'm sorry... Ben and Libby are in the den. You go on back."

Alex smiled and started that way, but she stopped in the entry and studied the elaborate staircase, draped with holly and silver bells. As usual, everything had been professionally decorated for Christmas. It looked beautiful, of course, but all Alex could do was compare the elaborate arrangements and embellishments to her mother's creations. Alex would have traded it all for just one of Selena's lopsided bows.

Closing her mind to the memories, she continued on her way and finally reached the open French doors that led into the den. The room stretched across the length of the house and looked out to the garden and pool. At one end, a massive rock fireplace took up the whole wall, a glowing Christmas tree—almost as large—filling up the other. When Alex entered, Libby rose from a chair beside the couch. "Alex! Come on in! I didn't hear the bell... Where's Gabriel?"

"Margaret shanghaied him. Last time I saw them, they were headed for the kitchen." Alex kissed Libby, then turned to the sofa. Ben was stretched out on the cushions, his face so thin and fragile-looking, it took away her breath. He smiled and held out his fingers in Alex's direction. His hand seemed almost transparent.

She hid her shock, or hoped she did, and brushed his cheek with her lips. "Merry Christmas, Ben."

He gripped her hand and wouldn't let go. "Merry Christmas to you, Lexie... You're truly a sight for sore eyes. We're so glad you could come over tonight."

He hadn't used her pet name in years and she felt her throat go tight. "Are you kidding?" she said lightly, sitting down beside him. "Nothing could have kept me away."

"Not even a new boyfriend?" His voice was weak, but his eyes twinkled. He wanted to let her know he'd accepted this change. "I'm anxious to meet him. Does he measure up to my standards?"

"I hope he does." She glanced at Libby, the obvious source of Ben's information, then returned her gaze to him. "But you'll have to be the judge of that."

"Tell me about him." Ben's teasing manner left him, his expression going sober. "Is he a good man?"

All at once, she didn't know what to say. *Was* Gabriel a good man? In the past she had definitely thought otherwise, but now the only thing she was sure of was her confusion.

Ben saw her hesitation and started to say something, but the squeak of Margaret's shoes announced her arrival, Gabriel at her side. Ben shot Alex a curious look then he looked over her shoulder.

Gabriel took Ben's outstretched hand in his, shaking it firmly but gently. The two of them exchanged a long, measuring look—the type men give each other when they both know the same woman—then Gabriel spoke. "Thank you for inviting me tonight. It's nice to spend Christmas like this." He tilted his head toward the roaring fire. "Our hearth back home wasn't that big, but it was always lit. It brings back some memories…"

At Gabriel's gracious words, Alex felt her shoulders ease. She'd been nervous about the two men meeting, but she shouldn't have been. Before long, they were talking so easily she left them alone and joined Libby beside the tree where gorgeously wrapped presents were stacked under its laden limbs.

Libby sent a glance toward the fireplace and the men before it. "Dad looks bad, doesn't he?"

"Yes, he does," Alex said. "But it seems as if he's enjoying talking to Gabriel."

"He couldn't wait for you guys to get here tonight. He really was anxious to meet Gabriel, just like he said."

Alex looked at Libby with a calm expression. Inside she was anything but tranquil. "And why is that?"

Libby reached out and removed an ornament on the

nearest branch. "I told him what I told you." Balancing the crystal globe in her hands, she met Alex's gaze. "That Gabriel loved you...and I knew you felt the same way about him."

Alex struggled to keep her reaction from her face. She and Gabriel had clearly played their roles too well, but oh, the possibility...

"Dad would have seen it for himself when you got here. I thought it was better to prepare him. I mean, you're probably, like, going to get married and everything, right?"

The idea sent Alex's head spinning. "Marriage is a huge step, Libby. It—it's not something we've discussed at this point. I'm not sure..."

Libby looked puzzled. "What's not to be sure about?"

"It's complicated," Alex answered lamely.

Libby waited for more, but the words wouldn't come and Alex gave up. "I can't explain it, Libby. You'll just have to believe me. Marriage is not where Gabriel and I are heading."

"But he loves you."

Alex took the delicate globe from Libby's fingers and hung it back on the tree. There was nothing more she could say; Libby had made up her mind.

GABRIEL HAD SENSED Alex's discomfort long before they arrived at the Worthingtons' house. He wasn't sure why she was so anxious, but as the evening wore on, she seemed to relax. By the time dinner had been served and they all—including Margaret—were heading back to the den to open the presents, she was actually smiling. He watched as she pushed Ben's wheelchair across the parquet floor. The older man laughed at something she said then reached up and patted her hand in a familiar way. Gabriel found himself wondering if she knew how much Ben still loved her.

They gathered near the twinkling tree. Gabriel took a chair to one side as Libby and Alex made a game of handing out the presents. The scene felt unreal to him. He couldn't remember the last time he'd spent the holidays in a home, surrounded by friends or family. Maybe as a child... But even then, the circumstances had been so dissimilar to this, he could have been on a different planet. Their only shared detail was the presence of the huge fireplace glowing at the other end of the room, just as he'd told Ben. But even that was fundamentally different. In this house, the fire was for atmosphere, the O'Rourkes had needed it for heat.

Libby clapped her hands, breaking his reverie. "Okay, everyone. Dig in!"

The sounds of rustling paper filled the room as Alex and Libby and Ben began to unwrap their presents. Alex stopped when she saw Gabriel sitting still. Pointing toward his feet, she said, "Aren't you going to open your presents?"

Gabriel had brought Ben an expensive bottle of wine, a Hermès scarf for Libby and a cookbook for Margaret, but he hadn't expected presents from them. He reached down for the nearest box, which turned out to hold brownies from the housekeeper. He thanked her profusely then lifted one out and ate it in two bites. She grinned at him, obviously delighted by his appreciation of her gift.

The other box was much smaller. He felt Libby's eyes on him as he picked it up and began to unwrap it. A moment later, he uncovered an intricately carved pocketknife nestled in the tissue.

"It's beautiful," he told Libby and then Ben. "This is a work of art—thank you so much."

"You have to pay us for it," Libby said with a sly smile. She took her dad's hand in hers. "Isn't that right, Dad?"

"Absolutely."

Gabriel looked at the two of them in confusion until Alex took pity on him and explained. "You should never give anyone a knife," she said, "or it will cut your friendship in two. Pay her a penny and you'll be fine."

Nodding his understanding, Gabriel reached into his pocket and searched through his coins until he found what he wanted. With a smile, he flipped it across the room to Libby and she caught it. "I've been carrying that around for some time," he said. "It's an Irish punt. Will that do?"

"It's perfect." Libby bent her head to study the coin then she jumped up and ran to Alex's side to show her. Gabriel watched her cross the carpet, and that's when it hit him.

There was something about the way she moved. Something about the way she held her hands. Gabriel didn't know what it was but at that very moment, staring at Libby Worthington, his jaw went tight and his mind flooded with a single image…

The image of a young woman in black, fleeing Alex's apartment.

ALEX WATCHED Gabriel watch Libby.

An unfamiliar expression suddenly darkened his face but he hid it so quickly, Alex was sure no one else noticed. Obviously feeling her gaze, he turned in her direction. A warning came into his eyes and she read it as clearly as if he'd spoken it. *Say nothing.* Swallowing quickly, she turned away. They finished opening their presents then she and Libby began to clean up. As Alex reached for a discarded bow beside Ben's wheelchair, she looked over at him.

He was trying his best to fight fatigue, but he'd begun to wane. Now his cheeks were too bright, his eyes almost feverish. Gathering up the last of the discarded paper and bows, she spoke. "We need to get out of here, Ben, and let you get some rest."

He rallied and tried to argue, but Alex rejected his pleas. Margaret bustled into the kitchen to prepare a box of food for Alex and Gabriel to take, then Libby and Gabriel went out to retrieve their coats.

"You don't need to leave." Ben tried one last time.

"You're tired," Alex said. "And you need to get to bed."

"Maybe so...but I don't want to."

Alex laughed. "You sound like Libby."

"She's doing a lot she doesn't want to these days. But I guess that comes with growing up...*and* with growing old."

Just as before, he held on tightly to her hand. "I like Gabriel, Alex. He *is* a good man. He'll take care of you."

"I don't need someone to take care of me anymore, Ben." Her voice was gentle. "Those days have passed. I take care of myself now."

"I know, I know." He nodded several times. "But that kind of taking care is not what I'm talking about."

She tilted her head. "What do you mean?"

"I'm not going to explain it right now," he said cryptically. "You're too afraid of loving him to understand."

She started to protest but Gabriel and Libby came back into the room. A flurry of goodbyes took place, then Alex and Gabriel went back out into the cold. She looked up at the sky as they drove down the driveway. Clouds had rolled in and they were pulling the moon across the darkened night. Ben's words echoed in her mind as Gabriel reached across the seat and took her hand. His touch blotted out Ben's baffling message.

But she'd remember it later and wonder how he knew.

GABRIEL LET HIS GAZE sweep the grounds of Alex's complex as they drove inside the gate and parked. Most of the residents had obviously headed out of town to celebrate the holidays—the place looked deserted. Satisfied with the way things appeared, he turned his eyes to Alex's profile.

She was staring out the car's window but her stillness told him she wasn't thinking of the scene before her. She was back at the Worthingtons', clearly worried over Ben's rapid deterioration. Gabriel had understood her quietness as soon as they'd gotten into the car, the realization keeping him silent as well, especially about his suspicions concerning Libby. He had no doubt Alex would immediately dismiss them, and he needed more time to think it through before he could defend the possibility. They entered the apartment a moment later and went through their usual routine, Gabriel returning to Alex's side at the front door after a quick reconnoiter.

She stood in the dark, a motionless shadow he could barely see. He brushed her face with a gentle touch, his fingertips playing across her cheekbones before he kissed her softly.

"You are incredibly beautiful," he whispered, lifting his lips from hers a moment later. "You do know that, don't you?"

She shook her head to deny his words, but Gabriel stopped her movement. Cradling her face between his palms, he stilled her with another kiss, this one even deeper.

They ended up in the bedroom.

Just as before, Gabriel told himself to walk away. But he gave the advice even less attention this time. Slipping the dark red jacket off Alex's shoulders, he kissed her bare skin, breathing in the scent of her perfume as he lowered her to the bed. He wanted to take it slowly so he could remember every second they were sharing; each caress they exchanged had to last him forever. Inching his fingers over her neck, stroking her back, tasting her secret places...he burned the sensations into his mind, but as he did so, his passion only increased. Too soon, his body demanded release.

This would be their last time together. It had to be.

Sensing the desperateness Gabriel felt but couldn't voice, Alex took control. Her hands and mouth connected with him in ways he would dream of later. Throughout it all, Gabriel did his best to slow the clock, but ultimately he failed. They came together in a rush of heated passion. The intensity of his desire was only surpassed by what he acknowledged a moment later.

He loved Alexis Mission.

He always had and he always would.

ALEX LAY in Gabriel's arms and listened to his heart beat. The rhythm was steady and strong, as reliable as the man it sustained. She knew now he *was* a good man, and she should never have blamed him for what happened to her family—he had only been doing his job—but she'd been too full of anger and grief to accept that ten years ago. The secrets he had kept, he kept because he had to...

But one truth remained.

He knew what had happened that day and she was still in the dark.

Looking up at him, she raised her hand and cupped his jaw. He gazed down at her with his unreadable eyes then put his hand over hers and squeezed. She'd traded her questions for his love, her suspicions for his protection. Her past for their present. Had the barter been a good one or a tragic mistake she'd always regret?

She put the question out of her mind and turned instead to something much less important, but which had bothered her nonetheless. "You watched Libby very closely while we opened our presents," she said softly. "What were you thinking?"

His expression closed and she knew immediately he was going to lie to her. She stopped him. "Don't tell me 'nothing,'" she said, raising herself up on her elbow to stare at him. "I saw you."

"I wasn't going to deny it," he said, staring at her.

"But you weren't going to tell me the truth…"

He shrugged. "I realized she reminded me of someone I used to know," he said after a moment. "Someone I'd rather not remember."

"A woman you loved?" Alex guessed, suddenly intrigued.

"Loved?" He shook his head reluctantly. "That wouldn't be the word I'd use."

"That you were involved with, then?"

"You're not going to give this up, are you?"

She smiled and shook her head. "I'm curious," she confessed. "Have you been married? Do you have any children? Have you ever had your heart broken?"

"No, no, and too many times to count."

"Did *she* break your heart? The woman Libby reminded you of?"

He stared at the ceiling. "No, she didn't break my heart. That would have been impossible."

"How come?"

"You have to *have* one to know how to break one. Toni was missing that vital organ."

He had answered her in a lighthearted fashion, but there was tension beneath the words. Alex wanted to ask him more, but his eyes told her she'd get nothing else. She let him pull her into his arms, and a moment later she no longer cared.

WHEN THEY WOKE AGAIN, it was way past midnight and officially Christmas Day. Alex wanted to give Gabriel the present she had for him, so she left the bed and went to retrieve it. Gabriel headed for his duffel. Digging into the bottom of the bag, he came up with the envelope he'd stolen the first time he'd been in Evan Frank's office. Staring at it and knowing what it contained, Gabriel realized he was losing his edge and doing something he shouldn't. A few weeks ago he would never have even remotely considered this, but a few weeks ago, he hadn't known Alex the way he did now.

Still, she continually surprised him. Her question about Libby had caught him off guard. He'd been hard-pressed to come up with a quick answer, but Toni had popped into his mind almost unbidden. Thinking about it now, he realized the two young women *did* remind him of each other, but most likely only because of their shared youth. Nothing else was the same.

Alex came in a moment later, holding a square, flat box wrapped in heavy paper. Climbing into the bed, she handed him the present. ''I'm anxious to see what you think of it,'' she said shyly.

Slipping his envelope to the side, he placed the package on his lap, then gently peeled back the heavy gold wrapping. When he opened the box, what he saw took him completely by surprise.

In his dreams, he'd seen the scene a thousand

times—but never through Alex's eyes. He held his breath and stared at the incredible painting.

She'd captured the purple and pink New Mexican sunrise as if she'd seen it that morning instead of ten years past, the colors so soft and delicate, he couldn't tell where one stopped and another started. Beneath the clouds, the mountains rose in silent witness, their snowcapped peaks barely visible through the early-morning vapor. He could smell the piñon trees and feel the biting wind. He'd never seen anything so perfect, so evocative...or so sad.

Grief hung over the entire image, so haunting and intense that it was visible in every brush stroke, a sorrow that would never go away. Using only paint and canvas, she'd managed to communicate exactly what she'd lost. Exactly what he'd taken from her.

"Do you recognize it?" she asked softly.

"Of course. It's New Mexico." He was unable to take his eyes from the painting. "The day I put you on the plane."

"The day my family died."

Unable to correct her, he studied the painting, details coming into focus. Details Alex had seen but to which he'd been blind. The winter greenery that fought the chill. The way the sun couldn't escape the clouds. The tinge of gold that gilded everything—not with a gleaming light but with an empty dullness.

"I don't know what to say. It's incredible..." His voice was hoarse as he looked up at her and he wondered if she knew how much of herself she had revealed.

She put her hand on his arm, her touch so gentle he could hardly feel it. ''You don't have to say anything, Gabriel. I understand. I didn't before...but I do now.''

And at that, something remarkable flowed between them. The emotion felt like forgiveness to Gabriel, but he rejected that possibility because Alex didn't know the truth and she never would. Therefore, she *couldn't* forgive him.

But looking into her eyes he suddenly realized it didn't matter. Catching whoever was after her wouldn't make things right between them, either. Nothing could do that.

Because what he'd taken from Alex—her family and her identity—was irreplaceable. He may have saved her life, but he'd also hurt her in an unbelievable way. By giving in to his desires to make love with her, he'd only compounded that injustice.

His da had been right. Gabriel *was* a bastard and Alex deserved better. It was time for him to go back to the real world. *His* world.

HE WAS TOUCHED by her gift—Alex could see that much by looking at Gabriel. But all at once, he left the bed and walked away from her. Puzzled, she stared at his back and started to speak. At the last minute, she stopped herself. Obviously something had disturbed him.

She looked at the painting and wondered if she'd misjudged. She'd thought the scene would mean as much to him as it did to her. She'd painted like a madwoman the past few days, pushing herself to finish the work in time for Christmas. She clearly shouldn't have bothered.

He stared out the blinds, then turned around. His expression was so cold and remote that he looked like a different person from the man who'd made love to her so tenderly.

"I have to leave," he said in a dispassionate voice. "There's something I need to do."

"Right now?" She looked at him in alarm.

"Yes." He reached for his clothing and dressed without looking at her, slipping an envelope, which had been on the bedside table, into the pocket of his jacket.

"I—I had a nice breakfast planned for the morning," she said stupidly. "Will you...come back?"

He answered vaguely. "I'm not sure how long this will take. Don't wait for me."

Her heart sank at his tone. She tried to put herself back behind the wall where she'd lived before his arrival, but she couldn't. Her protection had crumbled. "I don't understand, Gabriel. Did I...do something to offend you?"

"Of course not." His voice was sharp with all the edges it'd held the first time they'd met.

"Then why are you leaving?"

His hands stilled on the buttons of his shirt. After a pause so long it made her pulse stutter, he looked up. "I have to, Alex." He spoke more softly, but the finality was still there and she had no idea why.

He came to the bed and leaned over, his mouth finding hers to deliver a kiss she'd never forget. When he finished, he straightened up and looked at her. She felt as if he was memorizing her face, but then she realized she was doing the same. The penetrating eyes, the thick hair, the quiet intensity he wore like a coat he never removed...she grabbed each image and locked it away.

"Take care," he said, and then he was gone.

Alex sat numbly in the center of the bed and listened to the door close. He'd left the painting with her. And a broken heart as well.

CHAPTER FIFTEEN

NOTHING IN GABRIEL'S past experiences had prepared him for the pain he felt as he walked out of Alex's apartment. His heart was an angry wound, bleeding and raw.

He crossed the parking lot toward his car and Toni came back into his mind, something she'd once said haunting him. Despite her dark hair and sensual body, she'd been emotionally cold, withdrawn and remote.

"We're compatible because we're the same," she'd said one night, looking at him with her glittering black eyes. "We don't need anyone else, except to use them." At the time, he'd denied her accusation but now he had to accept it. He'd done nothing but use Alex ever since he'd met her.

Taking refuge inside his frozen car, Gabriel stared at the lights falling from the apartment's living-room window. He couldn't think about what had just happened, so he focused on the past. How he'd taken advantage of Alex was abundantly clear, but what about Toni? How had he used her?

The answer came quickly—she'd been gorgeous

and sexy and had made him feel twenty-five again. The minute she'd started heading for his table, his ego had inflated along with his dick.

But why him? he wondered all at once. What had he done for her?

In short, how had *she* used *him?*

He thought back to the time they'd spent together, to all the questions she'd had for him while at the same time keeping her own past a mystery. It'd been a contest to see which of them could reveal the least. He'd been suspicious at first, then at some point he'd decided she was too young to have that many secrets and he'd abandoned the game. But sitting in his darkened car now, cold and miserable, he mulled over the question in his mind, putting aside his current pain for his past. After a few minutes, a shadowy suspicion began to emerge.

And a cold chill came with it.

He gripped the steering wheel with both hands and tried to tell himself he wasn't thinking straight. It wasn't possible. Because of what had happened between him and Alex, he was losing his mind, letting his brain go too far. The idea didn't even make sense.

Or did it?

Cursing loudly, Gabriel started the car and wheeled into the street, punching out the numbers on his cell phone with one trembling hand, the other gripping the steering wheel.

Evan Frank answered on the tenth ring with an incredulous voice. "Tell me this isn't you…"

"I need some help."

"For God's sake, Gabriel, it's 2:00 a.m. on Christmas morning! I'm putting together my kids' new bikes!"

Gabriel had never known the man *had* a family. "I'm sorry, Frank, but I need to know—"

"If this is about the other women on the Mission case, I haven't had time to look into that yet. For now, I'm hanging up and you're on your own, buddy—"

"That's fine," Gabriel interrupted, "but if you don't meet me at the office, then I'm breaking in. I *have* to see something in the file. Something else."

"Breaking in—" The agent's voice rose with genuine horror. "Gabriel, no! They'll catch you and you won't see the light of day for a hundred years. It's too dangerous. You can't do that—"

"And if I don't, Alex Mission could die." The Toyota's wheels squealed around the corner. "I'll be there in five minutes," he said grimly. "You can help me or not, I don't care."

He ended the call and threw the phone across the seat, where it slipped down, unseen, between the cushion and the door. In the back of his mind, he hoped he was wrong, but something told him he wasn't.

ALEX JUMPED when the phone rang. Quickly setting the painting aside, she crawled across the bed and grabbed the receiver, praying Gabriel's voice would be at the other end.

It wasn't. Instead, a woman answered Alex's breathless hello.

"Is this Alexis Mission?"

The caller's voice was soft and muted and for some strange reason the first person Alex thought of was her mother. Then she realized who the woman had asked for—not Alex Worthington but Alexis Mission.

Alex gripped the phone and found her voice. "Who is this?"

"Who I am doesn't matter," the woman said. "Who *you* are is the question..." She paused. "But actually, I guess you don't need to answer that, either. I know already. And so do you."

Alex's throat closed. She couldn't say a word.

"I have some information you want...about your family. I know what happened to them and it's not what you were told."

"Who are you?" Alex whispered. "Why are you doing this? What do you want?"

"We've discussed the 'who,' and the 'why' doesn't matter. At least, not to you. As for what I want...you'll understand that later. Know this, though—" She let the silence build until Alex felt faint. "The man you've come to trust lied to you ten years ago and he's lying to you now."

"Wh-who are you talking about?" Alex stuttered. "I don't—"

"Don't tell me you don't know who I mean. If you're trying to get me to name him, that is a trick that will not work."

This time when the woman spoke, Alex caught a slight accent. "Tell me who you mean or I'm hanging up right now." It was an empty threat, but Alex had to do something to get back some control.

The woman was silent, then finally she spoke again, her answer not one to the question Alexis had asked, but an answer all the same. "He shares names with the Archangel but his power doesn't come from God."

Alex wasn't Catholic but she understood the reference. Gabriel the Archangel—the minion of God whose power came straight from the heavens.

"Why do you say that?" Alex asked the question without thinking.

"I know him and I know he is not an angel of goodness, but a killer of men." Her accent seemed to deepen then she caught herself. "I'm not calling to talk about him. Do you want to know what I have to say or not?"

"Of course I do, but—"

"Do you know the Tower? The one on the University of Texas campus?" She didn't wait for Alex to answer. "Meet me there on the observation deck. In fifteen minutes."

"It's Christmas!" Alex protested, glancing at her clock. "And almost two-thirty in the morning! The Tower can't possibly be open right now—"

"The doors will be unlocked. You won't be stopped."

Alex closed her eyes; this was crazy. If Gabriel had been there, he'd tell her it was too dangerous, a setup, a mistake…anything he could to stop her from going. And he'd probably be right.

But Gabriel was gone. He'd left her and taken his secrets with him. She was totally on her own, just as she had been before. If she didn't take a chance and meet this woman, Alex might *never* know the truth. The consequence of that would haunt her forever, even though she'd managed to convince herself it was no longer important.

"You're taking too long to decide." The woman sounded impatient. "I must assume you're not interested—"

"That's not true! But I need to know—"

"You need to know nothing, except this…" The woman waited so long to complete her sentence that Alex was afraid she'd hung up. Panic edged its way inside Alex's heart but then the woman spoke. "I don't just have information. I have your dark angel as well. Do you want to hear me kill him?"

A wave of dizziness hit Alex and for a moment she thought she was going to throw up. When she managed to get herself under control, she realized how improbable that was. Gabriel was too smart, too quick...too deadly. He'd never allow someone to grab him. "You're lying," she said in a voice that trembled anyway. "I don't believe you."

"I thought you might say that."

Alex heard a rustling over the phone and then Gabriel's voice. It was muted and in the background, but she recognized his deep-toned accent instantly. Her heart tumbled.

The woman came back. "You have ten minutes to get here. Come alone. If you're late, he dies."

GABRIEL REACHED for his weapon, looking neither right nor left as he headed straight for the Agency's doors. Before he got to the front steps, a second vehicle roared into the parking lot. Gabriel pivoted then watched as Evan Frank jumped out of his car.

With a loping run, the agent quickly covered the short distance to Gabriel's side. "I'm here," he panted. "I'm here. For God's sake, don't break the door down."

"I wasn't going to break it down." In spite of his words, a quiet relief flooded Gabriel at the sight of his friend. "I was going to blast off the dead bolts, then go in."

Taking out his keys, Evan Frank looked at him and rolled his eyes. "Wait here," the agent said. "I have to take care of the alarms first. Give me two minutes, then you can come up."

Gabriel nodded. He hadn't known how in the hell he was going to get inside, much less past the elaborate security system the Agency surely had in place. He would have figured out a way, but this was much easier.

A few minutes later, he was in Evan Frank's office.

"I need the Mission file," Gabriel said. "The whole one, too, not that thing you had in here the other day."

"How'd you know that wasn't complete?" Frank stared at him in amazement. "What'd you do? Go through it when I went to call the NYPD?"

Gabriel stared at him impassively. "I can get it myself, Frank—"

"No, no…" The other man stood. "I'll get the damn thing. We scan them now and keep them on disk. You just sit there and wait for me."

"Make it fast," Gabriel said as he left the room.

Five minutes later, Frank was back, carrying six CDs. He dumped them on the desk then bent over to boot up his computer, speaking as he stood. His irritation at being called on Christmas had given way to curiosity. "What in the hell is going on here, Gabriel?"

"I don't know," Gabriel answered in a grim voice. "But I have an idea, and to check it out I need to see the surveillance photos. Every shot we took of Guy Cuvier and his family. I want to see them."

Frank's eyes widened behind his glasses. "Gabriel, we've got hundreds of those, maybe thousands."

"Then I guess we're going to be here a while."

The computer on Evan's desk beeped to life, saving Gabriel from the agent's reply. Sitting down, he began to tap the keyboard as Gabriel dragged his chair closer to the monitor.

A collection of screens flashed by so quickly, he barely had time to register their content. He saw enough to know they were entering a secured database system, then Evan popped the first CD into his machine. More screens, then Evan turned to him. "Give me some keywords."

Gabriel stared at him blankly.

"Keywords," Frank said again. "What are you looking for, for heaven's sake? The Frenchman's dog or the kind of car he drove or—"

"His daughter," Gabriel answered, finally understanding.

"The kid?"

"That's right."

Frank lifted an eyebrow then began to type. A few seconds later, the screen flickered. "Nothing there," he said, shaking his head. "We'll have to try the others."

They were scanning the very last one when Frank spoke softly. "Bingo…"

Gabriel leaned in closer. A series of five tiny images bordered the page at the top. They were too small to see any detail, but Frank clicked on the first one, blowing it up on the twenty-inch screen. The photo was of Cuvier's wife and a young girl, who was maybe ten or eleven. Her face was barely visible behind her mother's figure. The agent closed that image and retrieved the next one. It was even worse, the back of her head the only part of her even in the frame. The third one was of the girl alone, but it'd been taken with a long lens. Shot through a window, the picture was blurry, almost useless.

The fourth one was perfect.

"Make it bigger," Gabriel commanded, staring at the terminal.

The agent obliged.

And a ghost whispered in Gabriel's ear.

"I can mess with it if you like," Frank offered.

When Gabriel didn't answer, Frank volunteered more. "You know, I can work on the colors, change her hairstyle, give her buck teeth—whatever you want."

Gabriel spoke haltingly. "Can you make her older?"

"Sure. How old you want her?"

"How old was she then?"

Frank narrowed his eyes and searched his own database. "Eleven?" he asked himself. "No, no...twelve." He looked up at Gabriel. "She was twelve."

"So she'd be twenty-two now..."

"That's right."

He'd thought her young, but not that young. Gabriel swallowed hard. "Make her twenty-two."

The agent started tapping the keys and humming, but Gabriel closed his eyes, already sick with the knowledge that he didn't need the computer's help.

He already *knew* what Antoinette Cuvier looked like. She was tall and curvy with long legs and black hair. She had a tiny tattoo on her right hip and a curved scar on her left ankle. She liked Thai food and she slept on her back. Naked. The last time he'd seen her they'd been in a bar, right where they'd started. "I'm moving on," she'd told him. "I've got things I have to do. You understand, don't you?"

He'd never seen the relationship as a long-term thing, but he'd felt relief at her pronouncement, without knowing why.

He understood now.

"Here she is," Frank announced. "Quite a looker, too."

Gabriel opened his eyes and stared at the face on the screen. She *was* quite a looker. That's why he'd taken her home. That's why he'd slept with her. That's why she'd lived with him.

"Antoinette Cuvier." Evan pronounced the girl's name then adjusted a knob at the bottom of the screen. The colors of her blouse muted just a bit. He spoke absentmindedly as he continued to fiddle with the control. "Old-fashioned name, but you never know what people are thinking when they name—"

Gabriel spoke thickly. "They call her Toni now..."

Evan Frank bobbed his head up and down, then he realized what Gabriel had said. His eyes rounded. "Holy shit...you know her?"

"No." Gabriel stood up, his excuse already forming. "I thought I did. But I was mistaken. This was a wild-goose chase." Slapping the agent on the back, he held out his hand. "Thanks, Evan. You've been a big help. Now go back and finish your kids' bikes..."

"That's it?"

Gabriel met the other man's puzzled gaze. He didn't need any help to do what he had to do now, but even if he had, he wouldn't have asked Frank for it. The agent was too good a man to get mixed up in this.

"That's it," he lied. "I can handle it from here."

ALEX DRESSED QUICKLY and ran out of the apartment, fright and apprehension overwhelming her as she started her car and raced toward the freeway. Who was this woman? Was she lying or telling the truth? She obviously knew enough to prove she had information about Alex's past, but what did she want? And why did she have Gabriel?

The unanswered questions accompanying her, Alex swerved off the interstate a few minutes later and took the Martin Luther King exit, heading for Guadalupe. At three hundred and seven feet, the Tower could be seen from almost anywhere in Austin, the huge clock a landmark all the residents knew. She found it quickly.

Within minutes she had parked and was racing through the deserted campus, her boots slapping against the frozen walkways. A flash of white against a holly hedge sent panic into her throat, but it was only a cat dashing across the path then disappearing. Moments later, Alex was at the doors of the Main Building, the base of the Tower.

Despite the woman's reassurance, Alex fully expected the entrance to be locked; she was shocked when the heavy doors swung open with a push. Within minutes she found the elevator and jabbed the button for the twenty-seventh floor. The car felt dark and rickety and she wondered if it could make it to the top. It did, the door opening after a lifetime. Alex stepped out and then there were stairs to climb. They twisted and turned, mesh doors with dangling locks between the landings. By the time she reached the pale green room that led to the observation deck, she was trembling and frightened. Taking a shaky breath, she searched frantically, darting around the elevator shaft that occupied the center.

But the room was empty.

GABRIEL SPED BACK to Alex's apartment, his heart pounding erratically. Antoinette Cuvier was her father's daughter, and like him, she would probably do anything to accomplish her goal, whatever it was. If he hadn't been so damn dense, he would have caught the resemblance to Guy. The dark Gallic eyes, the sharp cheekbones, the even sharper tongue. Gabriel had been so flattered by her interest, he'd removed his good judgment, along with his pants.

Their ''meeting'' hadn't been a coincidence because things like that didn't just happen. Somehow, somewhere, she'd found out about him and plotted the whole thing. It hadn't taken her too long, either. Only a few weeks had passed between the time Toni had moved out and when Alex had called him. Other questions bombarded him, but there would be time for answers later. Right now he had to find Alex.

He swung onto Oxford, but when he got to the complex the gates were closed. He slammed the Toyota against the curb, then ran to the metal fence surrounding the property. Two minutes later he was over the top and slipping through the shadows to Alex's apartment.

When he got inside, it was dark…and empty.

He wanted to scream with frustration but he didn't. Instead, he quickly searched the entire apartment. There was no sign of a struggle or forced entry. Alex hadn't packed any clothes, but she had taken her purse. He stood in the middle of the living room and thought. The list of places she might have gone was short. In fact, it only held one name. She *had* to be at Ben Worthington's house—she'd told Gabriel she had no close friends. Running to her phone, he pushed the speed-dial button labeled Ben. To his surprise, the call was answered immediately, Libby's voice offering him a shaky hello.

"This is Gabriel O'Rourke." He didn't bother with the niceties. "Put Alex on the phone."

"Alex?" Libby was clearly puzzled. "Alex isn't here, Gabriel. I was just about to call her, but then the phone rang—"

"Why were you going to call her? Did she phone you earlier?" He threw the questions at her. "Have you heard from her?"

His gaze fell to the phone as he waited for Libby's answer. Alex's caller ID button was blinking. She'd received a phone call sometime after he'd left. He reached out and punched the light and the number popped up on the screen followed by the word *Unavailable*.

"I—I was going to call her because my dad died," Libby said, her voice thickening as she drew his attention back to the phone. "Right after you left. He…he took a turn for the worse and we called the doctor, but there was nothing he could…"

Gabriel spoke automatically, his mind twirling. "Libby, I'm sorry… God…" He tried to concentrate but he couldn't. All he could think of was the number blinking up at him. The local area code was 512, so why would the number be unavailable to the caller ID? Saying the words he knew he should, he spoke again. "Is there anything I can do?"

"I appreciate the offer, but there's nothing right now. Where's Alex if she's not with you, though? I need to tell her..."

"I'm not sure." It'd worked before, so he tried the same excuse he'd used with the guard the other day. "We had a misunderstanding, and I left to cool off. When I returned, she was gone. I thought she might be there."

He paused in his excuse, comprehension coming all at once as he stared at the phone. The call Alex had received had to have come from a mobile phone. Mobiles couldn't always be identified, but the area code, if local, was recognized.

"I'm sorry, Gabriel, but she really isn't here."

"If she does call you, please tell her to get in touch with me."

"Of course. I'm sure she'd want to come here any-way. I—I'll tell her." Libby was clearly puzzled but too filled with grief and sadness to question him.

Gabriel immediately dialed the Agency. Frank an-swered on the first ring. "I'm on my way out the door, honey—"

"No, you're not," Gabriel said. "I've got a cell phone number and I need to know who owns it." He repeated the number twice, his voice so urgent the agent didn't bother to question him.

"I got it. Hang on."

For a lifetime, Gabriel waited, then Frank came back. "That was easy. The phone's in a rental car and—"

"And the car was stolen." Gabriel's gut tightened. "It's a white Lexus LS400, about a '95 or '96."

"1995," Evan answered. "Wow…give the man a cigar!"

"I'd rather have a name, or even better, a location."

"Impossible. But I can ask the locals to put out an APB on it. Would that help?"

No way was his first thought. Gabriel couldn't afford to get the police involved because it was going to get messy, even messier than before. Then he thought about the price he'd pay if he didn't find Toni Cuvier.

"Call them," he said hoarsely. "Give them my cell number and tell them it's an emergency…" He didn't have the right words, but Frank seemed to understand.

"I'm on it," the agent said.

Gabriel hung up the phone then turned back to the apartment and began to search it once more. There had to be something that might tell him where she'd gone. Five frustrating minutes later, the phone rang loudly, startling him.

"You're either the luckiest man on earth or you've been living right." Evan Frank's voice held amazement.

Gabriel's heart thumped. "What have you got for me?"

"A campus uniform spotted the car the minute the APB went out. He'd been called over to take a report—something about a missing security guard. The car's parked on Sixth Street, close to the Main Building. He's looking at it as we speak."

Gabriel grabbed his coat, talking and heading for the front door at the same time. "What's in the Main Building?"

"That's the Tower," the agent said. "You know...where the sniper hid in '66. He killed a bunch of people and—"

"How do I get there?" Gabriel interrupted.

Evan stopped his story and gave Gabriel directions. When he finished, Gabriel spoke again. "One last thing, Evan... Call that cop and tell him not to move. If I get there and that Lexus is gone, he's going to have a problem on his hands."

Without waiting for the agent's reply, Gabriel threw down the phone and ran out the door.

CHAPTER SIXTEEN

ALEX STARED at the empty room, disappointment swamping her. Then she saw a door.

She ran toward it and tried to push it open, but the wind pushed back, and it slammed the door shut right in her face. She tried once more and managed to get outside.

She was standing on an open deck and the view went on for miles. It was eerie and beautiful, terrifying and exhilarating. Running toward the ledge, Alex held her hair back with one hand and stared into the darkness. A safety structure stretched above her, but it didn't impede the view. Ransom Center loomed before her. She was facing southwest Austin, the hills beyond cloaked in darkness, the outline of Battle Hall a distant form. She twirled around to search the rest of the deck just as a woman stepped from out of the shadows.

She was much younger than she had sounded over the phone. Wrapped in a black coat with windswept hair to match, she came toward Alex with a slow and even step. Her face was composed of angles and lines, her cheeks bladed, her lips narrow. There was something jarring about the way she looked, something beyond her alabaster skin and otherworldly appearance. After a moment's study, Alex realized what it was: The girl's eyes were younger than the rest of her, as if the child she'd once been was still there but too frightened to come out.

"You're Alexis Mission," she said. Her voice was unexpectedly deep.

Chilled by what she saw, Alex stayed as she was, her back to the view. "Where's Gabriel? If you've hurt him—"

The girl dismissed Alexis's question with a wave of her hand. Alex's throat went dry as she followed the motion to the corner where a tiny recorder lay. She cursed, her mind racing. How on earth had this girl gotten Gabriel's voice on tape? Alex lifted her eyes. "Have you hurt him?"

The girl's eyes glittered. "Not yet."

"Who are you?" Alex said thickly, her panic growing. "And what do you want?"

The young girl shook her head. "You Americans… You're always in such a rush. Always straight to the point with no time for the pleasantries… I've waited a long time to meet you, and I like to do things slower. So we're going to do this my way."

The accent clicked and she suddenly understood the girl was French, a fact that meant nothing to Alex.

She moved slowly to Alex's right, circling until she

was standing beside the limestone wall. She threaded her hands through the security shell, her profile to Alex. "It's quite a view, isn't it? Can you imagine being up here and shooting all those people?" She cocked her thumb and pretended to fire a gun, turning slowly to Alex. "The bullet holes are still here, you know. You can see them—right over there."

Alex didn't take her eyes from the girl. "Tell me what you've done with Gabriel and what you want," she said evenly. "I'm not interested in sight-seeing right now."

"Neither was I," the girl said. "But my father insisted on bringing me and my mother with him to this country ten years ago. He had business here and he said we needed to see the world. He took us to New Mexico. To a miserable place they called Los Lobos."

Alex went still. The mechanical way the girl spoke was chilling, her lack of emotion even more so in view of what she was saying.

"My father supplied the global market with information. And he had business with *your* father, and your mother, as well. They were selling him secrets about the place where they worked."

Alex took an automatic step backward, the rough surface of the inside ledge hitting her side. She reached out and steadied herself. "You're lying. My parents were scientists and they loved their country—

they'd never do anything like that. They worked at a think tank—''

''And they were very good,'' the girl said. ''My father spoke of them often. To me, to my mother…to my uncle René. He said they had made themselves very rich because they were so smart.''

''No. No way. That's impossible.''

The girl went on as if Alex hadn't spoken, her recitation so perfect, Alex wondered how many times she'd told this story, if to no one else but herself.

''They weren't *that* smart, though. They got greedy. They wanted more money for their secrets, and when my father wouldn't give it to them, your father shot him.'' The girl paused as the wind shifted then died down and everything went quiet. ''*Your* father killed *my* father. He murdered him. In cold blood.''

Too appalled to respond, Alex stared at her in horror. After a minute she recovered enough to reply. ''My father would never have done something like that. My God, he'd carry a bug out of the house before he'd swat it—''

The girl took a step toward Alex, her hands in fists by her sides, her coat flapping open. ''I *saw* him,'' she said fiercely. ''No one knew I was there. They came to the house my father had rented. It was a huge place with a windowless basement. Whenever my father wanted to seem legitimate he would drag my mother and me out. Otherwise, when he conducted business, he would send us to the basement. It was dark and it smelled bad." She shivered, the memory obviously still a strong one. "I hated it when he made us go down there, and every time I could, I would escape. My mother was watching me closely that night, but I still managed to slip away in the confusion. I wanted to see what was happening... And I did. I saw it all."

Alex shook her head. "I don't believe you."

"I'm telling you the truth." Her voice rose. "Your mother was with your father and so was your little brother. Your angel came with them, too."

Alex wanted to argue, to scream, to refute the girl's story, but inside her head she heard Gabriel's version, his voice flat and deliberate. Who was telling her the truth? Who was lying to her?

"What did they look like?" Alex asked suddenly, her words gathering in her throat. "My mother... My brother... What did they look like?"

"Your little brother was blond, just a child. Your mother was the opposite—dark hair like mine. They were waiting in the car, a white van of some sort. I saw them when I snuck by, but they didn't see me. Later, she got out and I saw her better then."

"They were alive?"

"*Mais, oui.* All of them were alive." She spoke with a bitterness Alex could almost taste. "Your mother, your father, your little brother... They were alive and my father was dead. That's when your dark angel took over.''

Her description of Gabriel held contempt and something else that went much deeper. This girl knew Gabriel, Alex realized with a shock, and knew him well.

"He drove them away and never looked back. He left my father lying there, dead." Her voice returned to its monotone. "When I saw them leave, I came back to the house. My mother called my uncle, and when he came a few minutes later, I told him what had happened. He tried to find them, but it was too late. They were gone. And my life was never the same."

Stunned by the recital, Alex didn't know what to say. The girl's story was a fantasy—it had to be—but how did she know all the details? The things Gabriel had told Alex echoed inside her and her confusion grew.

The young woman stared out over the dizzying expanse, "When she heard the shots, your mother ran out of the van. She had on a red dress," she said almost wistfully. "And an apron. It had flour all over it and I wondered if she'd been baking. A crazy thing for a kid to think about in the middle of all this, no?"

Alex felt her mouth fall open. Her mother's favorite dress *had* been red and she would have worn it for the holidays. And she *had* definitely been baking— Alex could almost smell the lopsided pies that had been cooling in the kitchen that day. Suddenly she felt as if an elephant were sitting on her chest, keeping her from breathing. The girl turned to Alex and waited.

Several minutes passed before Alex could speak. Her face felt hot but she shivered. "My family is dead. They were all killed that night. It must have happened afterward and you didn't see it. They witnessed a murder and the killer came after them…"

"If that's what he told you, he lied." The girl put a strange emphasis on "he" and Alex knew she meant Gabriel. "Your father was the *murderer,* not the witness. And no one came after them. He took them away and they were very much alive. My uncle told me everything later. He said your angel worked for the government." She shrugged as if the matter were of no consequence to her. "Your family had served their purpose. I don't know, maybe he took them away somewhere and killed them all himself."

Alex stopped breathing. It wasn't as if she was holding her breath, but all at once she simply didn't need air. Turning her head, she looked into the endless expanse of the night. The sky felt so close she could have floated out and brushed it with her fingertips. She closed her eyes and thought of trying.

Had Gabriel killed her family?

In an instant she knew the answer.

No. Absolutely not. Gabriel O'Rourke had secrets—he'd lied to her and she'd always known it—

but he wasn't a murderer of innocent people. The hands that had touched her so intimately weren't the hands of a killer.

Opening her eyes, she shook her head. "Gabriel didn't murder my family. And *you're* lying," she said flatly. "I don't believe any of this."

The girl shrugged again and reached inside her long coat. Her hand came back out, gripping a knife. "I don't care if you believe me or not. I'm still going to kill you."

GABRIEL PULLED UP behind the Lexus and slammed on his brakes, stopping within inches of the expensive sedan's bumper. His eyes weren't on his driving because he'd just spotted Alex's car. With his pulse roaring, he jumped out of the Toyota. The campus cop was standing nearby, along with another uniformed man, a private security guard, Gabriel realized as he ran toward them.

Gabriel identified himself then spoke in a rush. "Where are they? The two women from those cars?"

"We haven't seen anyone." The UT cop, a young man with a crew cut and sharp eyes, answered Gabriel self-importantly. "I was told to stay here and watch the Lexus, so that's what I'm doing." He tilted his head toward the other man. "I originally came out on a call about a missing guard."

"One of our guys won't answer his radio." The uniformed guard was just a kid, his suit too big, his hair spiking in all directions. He looked scared and uneasy. Someone in a warm office had sent him out and he didn't know his ass from a hole in the ground. Words spilled nervously from him.

"He was supposed to be checking the Tower. We're short some folks this shift, being the holidays and all, so they sent Bill over to the Tower a while back. Now he won't answer the damn dispatcher..." He hitched up his pants and started to speak again, but Gabriel had heard enough. Antoinette had either bribed him to disappear, or more likely, eliminated him completely.

"Where's the Tower?" Gabriel growled. "Tell me! Right now!"

The kid raised a finger and pointed over Gabriel's shoulder. "Back there—"

Gabriel pivoted, then he saw it. The massive tower rose out of the darkness as if it were powered by a force of its own. At the very top, a columned open deck hovered above an enormous clock, ringed in gold. He set off into the darkness at a dead run.

"I DON'T UNDERSTAND." Alex spoke calmly, quietly. There was no hint of her fear in her voice, no tinge of fright in her words. All of that was swirling inside her but she kept it to herself. "Why do you want to kill me? What good would that do? It won't bring back your father..."

"That's not the point of this exercise."

"Then what is?"

"It's called revenge." The girl stepped closer to Alex. "You don't read your Bible too often, do you? 'Whoever sheds man's blood, by man shall his blood be shed.' Genesis 9:6."

"But I didn't kill your father."

"No, your father did, and my uncle took care of him, but I promised my mother we would have our revenge another way. For my father's *and* for my uncle's deaths." Her voice shifted, something in it even more ominous than before. "I'll have to find your angel for René's sake, but that won't be a problem. I know where he lives."

Alex stared. "You believe Gabriel killed your uncle?"

"I know he did. He hunted him down like a dog and shot him."

"But why? That makes no sense—"

"Believe her," a deep voice commanded from out of the darkness. "She's telling you the truth, Alex. I did kill her uncle and I'd do it all over again if I had a second chance."

Gabriel stepped out of the darkness, a gun in his hand.

Distracted by his appearance and shocked by his words, Alex never saw the girl move. In a flash, she was at Alex's side, the knife in her hand now against Alex's throat.

"Drop it, Toni," Gabriel said quietly. "She had

nothing to do with what happened. Your argument is with me.''

Alex's face was an ashen oval floating against the dark backdrop of Toni's coat. She looked shattered, her eyes huge, her hands locked on the younger woman's arms. She started to say something but Toni pressed the knife closer and broke skin. Alex gasped, and a trickle of red, like a single tear, instantly flowed down her slender neck.

Gabriel kept his expression neutral but on the inside he was screaming. The minute he'd found the body of the dead guard stuffed behind a desk downstairs he'd known something had gone terribly wrong. The unlocked doors had led him upstairs.

"Silence!" Toni hissed. "I want no more of your *merde!*"

Gabriel moved a step closer. His progress was so infinitesimal and smooth, Antoinette didn't notice. *"I* killed René,'' he said calmly. "Deal with me.''

Her eyes narrowed in a chilling way. "I will,'' she said, "but *this* is for my father.'' She jerked Alex backward. "Don't lie and say you killed him, Gabriel, because I was there. I was a child, but I know what I saw. Her father killed my father. I saw him pull out the gun and shoot him. I was there.''

Gabriel's shock was momentary, comprehension replacing it. That's how she'd known... He started to ask if she'd seen her father's gun come out first, then he stopped. She wasn't at a point where reason meant anything.

He sent Alex a look of silent apology, then focused once more on the younger woman. "Robert *did* kill your father, but only because of me," he said. "*I* brought him and his wife into the mission. They were amateurs and I used them because I knew I could. They weren't responsible for what happened. I am." He took another step. "I set up everything. It was all my fault…"

He stared at Alex and she stared back, her fierce gaze burning two holes into his soul. Then Toni tightened her hold and took two more steps backward, dragging Alex along. Alex stumbled as they hit the wall and cried out, the knife flicking against her skin a second time, a faster rush of red accompanying her cry.

All he wanted to do was shoot, but at this angle and with this weapon there was no way Gabriel could hit Toni and miss Alex. Toni was trapped, though. There was nowhere for her to go. Sooner or later she would try whatever she was going to try and he would make his move.

He risked a glance behind the two women, his gaze flicking outward. For a second he thought he was imagining things, then he realized he wasn't. His heart stopped its frantic pumping and everything inside him went cold.

The protective covering above the ledge had been

cut, and a huge hole gaped open. There was nothing between the women and the ground, more than three hundred feet below.

Gabriel jerked his eyes back to Toni and she smiled at his understanding.

With her knife at Alex's throat, she forced Alex to climb to the top of the limestone wall. Gabriel watched in horror as they tottered in the darkness.

"DON'T DO THIS," Alex pleaded. The girl's chest was pressed against Alex's back and Alex could feel her sharp breaths. She had one arm wrapped under Alex's breasts and the other around a nearby support. How she kept her grip on the knife, Alex didn't know, but she could feel the tip pressing into her throat. "We can help you," Alex said desperately. "We can talk about—"

Her answer was hot on Alex's neck. "I don't want your help. I want your blood on my hands and then I'll go to hell happy."

Below them, the lights of Austin danced dizzily. Alex closed her eyes and tried not to sway. She'd managed to tangle her own fingers into some wire hanging nearby, but her grip was tenuous and painful, the sharp points piercing the flesh of her palms. "Don't do it," she whispered hoarsely. "It's not worth it—"

The knife went deeper and Alex felt faint at the white-hot sting that came with it. "Don't say that!"

the girl ordered angrily. "I've lived my life wanting you dead. Your father destroyed my family and someone has to pay!"

The pain-filled words reverberated deep inside Alex. She understood exactly what the girl was saying because she'd felt the very same way, but about Gabriel. Then she'd come to love him. Now, it seemed, they'd gone full circle. He'd recruited her parents? He'd used them? Had he killed them as well? She turned her eyes in his direction, her gaze skewering his.

His stare pleaded with her for understanding, but she couldn't give it to him. She spoke again to the girl behind her, her double meaning clear.

"I agree with you," Alex said. "Someone *should* pay for what happened. I understand."

Her words didn't surprise Gabriel, but they did shock the girl. Alex could feel her hold ease minutely...then it tightened again. "You don't understand anything about me," the girl whispered. "You can't. No one can."

Without any warning, she let the knife fall from her hand. The sharp blade clattered to the limestone where it bounced once and then went over the wall. Alex watched the silver twist in the wind until it was swallowed by the darkness. When she lifted her gaze, Gabriel was in front of her, holding out his hand.

Alex reached for him.

Their fingertips brushed, then Toni snatched Alex back, wrapping her arms around her in a deadly embrace. Launching herself backward, she took both of them into the void below.

CHAPTER SEVENTEEN

HE READ HER EYES a moment before she moved.

Gabriel lunged forward, a twisting, folding fear rippling down his spine. His fingers found air and then something else. He gripped blindly, refusing to let go as the wire sliced into his leather coat and then his arms.

"I've got you!" he cried. "Hang on!" His fingers cramped but he managed to get his other hand over the wall as well. He pulled with every ounce of strength he had, and Alex's white face appeared. He had the left shoulder of her jacket in his hand. When he looked around her, he saw Toni as well. She was hanging on to Alex's waist.

Behind him, Gabriel heard the clatter of the open door, then running footsteps. Help had finally arrived, but Gabriel couldn't wait. Bracing against the weight of both women, he gritted his teeth and jerked his arms upward. The sockets of his shoulders creaked then popped, and for just a second he thought he might lose them both.

But Alex had reached the edge. She dug her hands

into the limestone and pulled herself up, her breath rasping in the cold night air as she struggled to climb back onto the deck. The cop Gabriel had heard arrive ducked under his side and helped Alex while Gabriel leaned out and reached for Toni. Clutching the corner of her sleeve, he began to lift her up.

When they were eye to eye, Antoinette looked at Gabriel and then she looked beyond, seeing something he prayed to God he never would. A second later, she lifted her feet to the wall and pushed herself away, ripping her coat from his hands.

Gabriel cried out, but Toni stayed silent all the way down.

GABRIEL GAVE his explanation, curt and tense, to the local authorities, who accepted it with only perfunctory questions. Evan Frank's appearance had something to do with that, Alex was sure, but the Austin detective who came to the scene had already received a phone call, he said, his gaze measuring Gabriel carefully. Everything would be handled, he assured them, including the gun they'd found in the Lexus, obviously the weapon Toni had used when she'd tried to break into Alex's apartment. A map to the YMCA had been there as well.

Gabriel and Evan Frank huddled briefly, then Gabriel insisted on Alex going to Seton. She let him drive her to the nearby hospital where she was stitched up. An hour later, they were back at her apartment. Alex was numb, both emotionally and physically, but she couldn't put off her questions. Not after all this. Not any longer.

She sat down on the couch and closed her eyes, horror and disbelief swirling inside her. After a bit, when she'd managed to box the images and file them away, Alex looked up at Gabriel. His eyes were flat and so was his expression, but she refused to be intimidated by either.

"You knew her, didn't you? You figured out who was after me and then you made the connection..." Alex didn't wait for an answer. "How did you realize it was her? How did you know to come to the Tower?"

He explained his trip to Evan Frank's office, then how he'd returned to Alex's apartment. Pausing after a moment, he spoke again. "Toni came on to me at a bar a few months back. I had no idea who she really was, but before I knew it, she'd moved in with me."

Alex nodded. "That's how she had the recording of your voice."

"She must have made it then. I had no idea..." He shook his head. "But how she knew who I was and located me may be something I'll never know. René must have told her, I don't know..."

"She used you to find me."

"Yes."

"Tell me," Alex said after a minute. "Tell me the truth. All of it. From the very beginning..."

He nodded but said nothing. After a moment he went into the kitchen then came out with two tumblers. She took the ginger ale but didn't drink, watching him instead as he emptied his glass but for a few sips.

"Sometime after you left for Peru, I recruited your parents for the Agency," he said wearily, sitting down on the couch. "I needed people on the inside to catch a bad guy we'd been unable to trap." He lifted his eyes. "For years, Guy Cuvier had been selling U.S. technology to anyone who would buy it, and it had been my job to stop him. I had failed miserably, and I was getting desperate."

He set his glass down on the cocktail table and scrubbed his face with his hands as if he could wash away the story. When he dropped his fingers, his stare was empty.

"Your parents were very willing to help. They loved their country and said they'd be happy to do whatever they could as long as their family wasn't endangered." He looked at the glass on the table. "I assured them that wouldn't be the case."

He was silent for a moment, then spoke once more. "We were very close to reeling Cuvier in. Your parents had made contact with him on several occasions and he was getting comfortable with them. When he called on Thanksgiving Day and wanted to meet with Robert, they assumed something important had come up. They called me and I drove them out there in the van, the same one I took you away in. They had Toby with them—his baby-sitter wasn't home and Selena wouldn't let Robert go alone.''

Alex's heart clenched. That sounded exactly like something her mother would do.

"We went to Cuvier's house and your father went inside.'' Gabriel's voice deepened as he recalled the details. "The two of them began to talk about the deal, but before I could figure out what was going on, Cuvier had pulled a gun.'' Gabriel looked at her bleakly. "I went for my weapon as Cuvier fired, but your father was faster. He killed Guy Cuvier. I swear I didn't know Robert even had a gun or I would never have let him go out there.''

Alex went cold and then numb. Toni *had* told her the truth. Alex's father *had* killed Guy Cuvier... It didn't seem possible, yet she had no doubt; she could tell from Gabriel's voice that she was finally getting the truth.

"I grabbed him and your mother and Toby, threw them into the van and took off. I had to get them out of there as quickly as possible, which wasn't easy since I obviously hadn't been expecting anything like what had happened. I called for a cleanup team but the nearest one was in Santa Fe. It took them a while to get there.''

She interrupted him. "A cleanup team?''

"That's what we call them...'' He seemed reluctant to explain. "It's a group of people who come into a situation only after things have gone wrong. They do whatever they have to in order to...clean up the problem."

He continued when she stayed silent. "I secured your family, and then I went to the house. Your mother had warned me you might come home. When I got there, I realized you had arrived, so I waited for you."

"You 'secured my family'? I take it that means they were alive at that point."

"Yes." He didn't blink. "They were alive and I got them out on a chopper. Before they left, they gave me their wedding bands and told me to give them to you, which I did."

Once again, he waited for her to comment, but Alex had nothing to say. A huge emptiness had opened up inside her. She felt hollow and vacant.

"Sometime during those hours, René Cuvier learned what had happened," Gabriel continued.

"Toni saw the shooting," Alex said in a wooden voice. "She told her mother and she called him."

Gabriel nodded. "René must have gone immediately to your house but no one was there. You either hadn't arrived yet or you'd come then left to go looking for your mom and dad." Gabriel frowned. "He must have seen something at the house—I suspect the photo you wanted to take—and realized you existed. I don't know how, but he followed your trail, because we know he went to the think tank then to the gas station.''

''Where he killed the attendant…''

''That's right.''

He leaned back against the sofa.

''So what happened to them?''

Her question was a simple one, but Gabriel didn't answer. Instead, he aged before her eyes, his face taking on lines she'd never seen before, his gaze going vacant.

''What happened to my family?'' she repeated. ''My brother, my mother…my father? How did they die?''

''René Cuvier tracked down your father and killed him.''

Fresh grief gnawed at her heart, but she kept the pain inside. ''And then you killed Cuvier.''

''I had to. If I had let him live, he would have gone on until he'd killed everyone else.''

Her throat closed up, but somehow Alex managed to speak. ''Everyone else?''

''You,'' he said. ''And your mother and your brother.''

''They were still alive?''

His eyes appeared full of pain yet she knew that

couldn't be the case. "Yes," he said slowly. "They were alive then. And they're alive now."

ALEX'S EXPRESSION changed so slowly he wasn't sure she'd heard him. "They're alive?" she said incredulously. "Right now? Both of them?"

"As far as I know."

She sat as if paralyzed, her hands curled in her lap, her gaze unwavering from his. Then she spoke. "You bastard."

"I had to—"

Exploding off the couch, she screamed at him, her glass flying to the carpet, ginger ale going everywhere. "My mother and brother are alive and you never told me? Don't you know what that means to me? All this time I could have been with them—I would have found them—"

He took a step toward her but she held out her hand and stopped him. "I made a promise I would keep you safe," he said. "I couldn't have done that if I'd told you they were alive. You would have—"

"I would *never* have told anyone. I would have died before I—"

"You're damn right you would have died." He interrupted her, his voice as harsh as the reality they were discussing. "Cuvier's people would have tortured you until you told them, then they would have killed you, found them and killed them, too. I couldn't risk it."

"You could have told me they were alive at least!

If I hadn't known where they were, I couldn't have told!''

''And would you have been content with that, Alex? Would you have let it be?'' He shook his head, the words spilling out too fast to contain. ''Don't bother to answer that because you and I both know the truth. You wouldn't have rested until you'd found them, and they knew that! That's why your father insisted I tell you they were dead. He knew it was the only way he could keep you alive. It was his decision, Alex, not mine. His. I didn't agree, but I did what he wanted because I owed him that, at the very least. I told you they were dead so you wouldn't go looking for them.''

''I don't believe you,'' she whispered. ''My father would have never done that to me. He loved me…''

''And *that's* exactly why he did it. If you don't believe me, then ask your mother. She agreed with him.''

''Where is she?''

''I have no idea.''

The room vibrated with tension and anger. Alex came closer to him, her eyes swimming with tears she refused to let fall. He thought she was going to strike him, but she spoke instead, her words so painful he would have welcomed a slap.

''How could you do this to me?'' Her voice broke. ''How could you hold me in your arms and make love to me? Did I mean so little to you? Was what we shared so unimportant that my pain didn't matter?''

The apartment fell silent, save for Gabriel's heart. Inside his chest, it was self-destructing, beat by horrible beat. He couldn't tell her the truth because she wouldn't believe him. Not now. Not ever. Trying to make it easy for her, he looked at her and lied one last time.

"What we 'shared' was your bed, Alex. There was nothing more than that between us. You know it and so do I."

"You're a bastard," she said again.

He nodded in agreement. "You're absolutely right."

A WEEK PASSED, then two. Alex spent as much time as she could with Libby, but she wasn't much use. Ben's dying had hit his daughter as hard as Alex had expected, and she was oblivious to Alex's own state of mind or her vague attempts to help. All Alex could remember were Ben's final words to her.

He'd said Gabriel was a good man and she should let him protect her.

She'd gone to the grave site and told him how wrong he'd been. Staring at the headstone, Alex felt more abandoned and lonely than she'd ever felt before. The day Gabriel had walked out of her apartment she'd started searching for her brother and mother, but after just a month, she knew it was going to be tough. Finding people who had disappeared ten years ago was a formidable task.

She finished the quarter at Claiborne, but when

March came, Alex handed her resignation to Randy Squires, her failure so far giving way to determination. He tried to talk her out of leaving the academy, insisting she meet him for dinner, where he begged her to stay. When she remained adamant, he then begged her to tell him what was wrong. She got up and left, leaving him sitting by himself at the best table in Emilia's.

When three more months had passed and she'd still had no success, Alex didn't know which way to turn.

Standing one night in front of an empty canvas at the end of another frustrating week, Alex groaned and threw her paintbrush down. A streak of pale blue appeared on the wall beside her, and then the brush tumbled to the floor, spreading the paint into the nap of the carpet. She sat down heavily on the ruined rug, the hot sting of tears filling the back of her throat.

The one thing she'd always been able to count on—her talent—had now abandoned her, too. Haunted by the night in the Tower and Gabriel's dark eyes, she hadn't been able to paint since everything had happened. Leaning her head against the wall, Alex closed her eyes and faced the truth she'd been avoiding for months.

She wasn't going to find her mother and Toby.

Gabriel had betrayed her.

She was on her own.

The choices were slim; she *had* to do something drastic or she was going to lose what was left of her mind. Touching the scars at her wrists, she tried not to tremble, but she could already feel herself slipping away, sliding down into that empty space where she'd disappeared all those years ago. She had no control over anything and the darkness was calling her.

She dropped her head to her knees, then the idea came without warning. She didn't stop to think about it or analyze what it meant. She simply went to the phone and called the airline. Two days later, she was in Peru.

GABRIEL SAT at the bar and watched the bartender tease the parrot. In the time that had passed since he'd fled the hotel to rush to Alex's side, nothing had changed.

Yet everything was different.

He felt like an amputee who'd woken up from surgery and was missing something vital. He knew he needed it, but he just couldn't figure out what it was.

He couldn't figure it out because he didn't want to. The painful reality was too awful to confront so he didn't. He drank and he fished and he watched the bartender and the parrot… He didn't allow himself to think about Alexis or what had happened between them.

ALEX HAD FORGOTTEN how clean and crisp the Peruvian evenings could be. Standing on the quiet street, she took a deep breath and watched a youngster tend a donkey. He was supposed to be herding the animal home, she was sure, but they weren't going to get there anytime soon. Which probably wouldn't matter anyway, Alex thought. No one was in a hurry here. She'd forgotten about that, too.

Turning away, Alex headed back for the room she'd rented at a small *casa de huéspedes*. She'd planned on staying for a while, but Pricaro had changed, despite the boy and the donkey. Ancient ruins had been found in the nearby mountains, and the town now had tourists. When she'd been there, the settlement had had one unreliable phone. Now there was cable TV. She didn't care for the foreigners, although she *was* one, and she didn't like the way the people depended on them. Where was Esteban now? He'd wanted to help the locals have a better life. Was this what he had defined as better?

The questions occupied her mind as she walked through the dusky streets, which was exactly why she'd come to Peru. Without even knowing it, she'd needed to leave her surroundings to forget about Gabriel and everything that had happened. She told herself it was working—but she hated to go to bed. She dreamed every night of a faceless man with Gaelic eyes and warm hands.

She reached the tiny boardinghouse with its brightly painted adobe walls and red-tiled roof and swung open its double doors. Once inside the shaded courtyard, she took off her hat and fanned her face. Even at night, Pricaro was humid and hot.

The woman who owned the *casa*, Señora Martine, bustled forward as the gate squeaked shut. They went through this routine every evening after Alex's walk, so she wasn't surprised to see the older woman. They greeted each other politely, then Alex sat down in the courtyard. A *café con leche* appeared a moment later and she smiled her thanks. Alex sipped the coffee and watched the moon rise over the rooftops. When the cup was empty she headed for her room. Ten minutes after that, she was in her bed and asleep.

Just like that night in the apartment, she didn't know what woke her.

Her pulse pounding, her throat dry, Alex slipped out from beneath the covers and walked to the deep-set window. The courtyard was as bright as daylight...and completely empty. She turned around to go back to bed but a movement caught her eye. Looking closer, Alex froze as the silhouette of a woman took form in the silvery shadows. Thinking of Toni Cuvier, she caught her breath before she remembered.

Toni was dead.

But this woman was not.

''Oh my God...'' Alex whispered the words, but the shimmering ghost heard her. She looked straight at Alex then lifted her finger to her lips as if to tell her to be quiet. Alex nodded then flew into her mother's arms.

CHAPTER EIGHTEEN

THEY TALKED FOR HOURS, their voices as quiet as the doves that whispered in the trees above them. Alex couldn't believe her eyes and neither, it seemed, could Selena.

"You're so beautiful," she kept saying. Touching Alex's face, her mother wept. "I can't believe it...I just can't believe it."

"How did you find me?" Alex asked. "I looked everywhere once I learned the truth, but—"

"I knew you were looking," Selena said. "But I had to pick the time and the place for us to meet. For you, it is all right, but it is not safe for me, Alex. Even now. There are people like the Cuviers everywhere."

"But you're not involved anymore! You're not—"

Selena reached out and put her fingers over Alex's lips. Her voice was fierce. "I have obligations..."

Alex regarded her mother in shock as comprehension slowly dawned. "Oh my God! You still work for the Agen—"

More quickly than before, Selena cut her off again, her touch more firm. "I want you to go home and live your life," she said. "Your father and I made the sacrifice we did so you and your brother could live. Do not waste our gift."

It was too much to absorb at once. Alex stared at her mother in disbelief. "Toby...Toby's not with you?"

Pain flashed through Selena's eyes. "No. I let him be adopted, Alex. When your father was killed, I realized how dangerous these people were and I could not risk Toby's life, too. He lives in the States. He is happy. He—he is good." Her voice cracked, and Alex caught a glimpse of the nightmare her mother had lived.

She composed herself quickly, an inner strength guiding her that hadn't been there when Alex was younger. "I saw him last year. I—I had learned he was sick. I went to the States and even to the hospital where he was. He recovered, but once I had seen him, I couldn't stand it. I had to see you as well. That's when I went to Austin. To your apartment. I picked the locks and went in. I took your drawing." She blinked and looked away. "I keep it somewhere safe. When I can, I look at it."

It *had* been her mother in the apartment that night! Alex was relieved, but at the same time still troubled. "Where is Toby?" she asked. "I want to see him—"

"No!" Selena gripped Alex's arm with surprising strength. "You cannot contact him, Alexis. Never! Do you understand me? He's happy where he is and we have to leave him there! I won't tell you where he lives…"

Alex tried hard not to understand but she failed. Her mother was right—Toby had been untouched by what had happened and he needed to stay that way. She wanted to ask more questions, but Selena spoke again, her fingers still wrapped around Alex's arm.

"You've got to find Gabriel," she said. "And make your peace with him. He's the reason you're alive today, Alexis. He came to you when you needed him most, and you owe him everything—"

"You know about Gabriel? How did you—"

"I know everything." She spoke in a way that allowed no more questions. "But you do not. Gabriel is a good person. He—"

Alex made a sound of disgust. "He almost got me killed—"

"No! He saved your life, Alex. He didn't just come when you called him. He has been watching over you ever since your father and I left. He has been your guardian angel, and you never even knew it."

"He told me that, but—"

"He promised your father he would take care of you and he has. I *know* this for a fact. I have watched him and he has watched you."

"He's the reason our family fell apart," Alex argued. "He's the reason—"

"He is the reason you and your brother and I are all still alive." Selena paused. "And he loves you," she added almost reluctantly. "He has loved you for years. I saw him fall in love with you bit by bit, day by day."

"No..." Alex shook her head. "You're confused, Mother. That can't be the truth. He betrayed me—"

"He loves you," she insisted. She paused and then her expression softened. "And you love him. Don't be foolish, Alex. Go to him. Let him take care of you. Tell him what's in your heart."

In the moonlight, Alex stared at her mother, something twisting deep inside her. "I—I don't know what's in my heart," she said finally.

"Yes, you *do* know. You just don't want to accept it." Selena's eyes filled with a mother's understanding. "He is a wonderful man, Alexis. And you can trust him. Let him love you, sweetheart."

SELENA WAS GONE when the moon went down. The next day Alex left Pricaro and headed for Lima. Two days later she was back in the States. When she walked off the plane and into the busy Austin airport, she felt as if the trip—and meeting her mother—had been a dream.

But it wasn't. A dream wouldn't have changed the way Alex felt about everything. Somewhere between

Peru and Texas, flying silently through the endless sky, her heart had begun to accept the truth. Molded by her mother's words and some other process to impossible to define, Alex had come to accept her deepest fears and rawest longings. Gabriel O'Rourke *was* a good man. And, just as Ben had said, Gabriel was the man who could take care of Alex. Not in the old-fashioned sense, but in the way that she needed the most.

He made her feel safe. He made her feel loved. He would *never* abandon her.

She got in her car and wondered if she'd ever be able to tell him how she felt.

SHE OPENED THE DOOR then dropped her keys on the table and a small duffel on the carpet. She'd been gone for some time, but he'd waited.

He could do nothing else. Alex was the part he'd been missing, and when he'd finally given in and acknowledged that truth he'd known what he had to do. She jerked her gaze to the corner where he sat, but he stayed silent.

For a time that felt like eternity, they just looked at each other. Finally, standing slowly, Gabriel walked across the room. He lifted one finger and drew it down her cheek, his hand falling to his side. His voice was hoarse and unsteady. "Can you ever forgive me?"

She seemed to hold her breath then she let it out slowly. "No...I can't forgive you, Gabriel."

An aching emptiness filled him. She started to speak again, but he put a finger across her lips. "I understand," he said. "I can't forgive myself, so how could I expect you to ever forgive me?" He shook his head, then cupped her jaw, rubbing his thumb over her bottom lip before dropping his hand once more.

"You don't understand." She reached out and took his hand in hers. "I can't forgive you...because you did nothing wrong."

Disbelief washed over him, a wave so strong he felt himself sway.

She shook her head. "I'm the one who should ask for forgiveness, Gabriel. I blamed you when I should have thanked you. I didn't understand until I found my mother and talked with her. Then I realized I hadn't been fair to you. I—I'm not even sure why you did everything you did. I don't deserve it..."

In another time and place, he might have left at that point, turned away and walked into the darkness by himself. Those days were behind him, though.

"I did it because I love you," he said. "I always have. I had to come back and tell you that, regardless." He reached inside his leather jacket and pulled out a white envelope, handing it to her. "I had to come back and give you that, too. It's your Christmas present."

In the dim light falling through the blinds, she

slowly opened the envelope. She looked inside and lifted out the photograph it held. It was the one he'd ripped from her hands the night they'd left Los Lobos. Ten years ago he'd put it in the file, and he'd stolen it from under Evan Frank's nose.

Alex stared at it, the column of her throat moving as she swallowed back her tears. Finally, she spoke. "You'll never know what this means to me," she said quietly. "Never."

He did understand—that's why he'd taken it for her—but he kept that to himself. "I didn't want to hurt you, Alex. All I wanted to do was protect you. And save your life."

"And you did," she said. "More times than you know."

He studied her face, her eyes, her hair. Every detail seared itself into his brain. He held his breath.

"I've been a fool, a terrible fool," she said.

"Forget forgiveness," he said hoarsely. "It's not important anymore. Give me your love. That's all I want."

She put her arms around him and held him fiercely. "You have it," she said. "Along with my faith and my trust and my very life—you have it all. For now and for always."

EPILOGUE

STARING INTENTLY, the slender woman stood just outside the chain-link fence, her fingers clutching the wire, her blond hair whipping about her face. She could have been the mother of any of the uniformed boys kicking the soccer ball up and down the grassy field before her. A quiet man waited beside her. He was motionless, a steady rock, his hand resting on her shoulder in a reassuring way.

She looked up at the man and motioned toward the field. He followed her movement with his eyes. One of the boys, the goalie, stood out. He was taller than the others and slim, his teenage body not yet filled out. His brown hair was darker than the woman's but if she'd been closer she would have seen her father's eyes in the young boy's face.

The man nodded once, confirming the woman's unspoken question. She'd been looking for the boy for a long time and the man had found him for her. She could get no closer, though. The boy had no clue of his former life, no idea of what had happened to him before his memories could be formed. On the other side of the fence, another man and woman watched. They were the only family the boy knew and it had to stay that way. To protect him and all the people who loved him. She'd had to see him, though. She'd had to put the final piece in place in order to go forward.

The woman at the fence watched a little longer, then she turned. The man at her side wrapped his arms around her and held her tightly. His embrace was protective and caring, a shield that had been forged by an unforgiving past and polished by a love so deep it defied expression. After a moment, he lifted her chin and kissed her, and then they walked away together.

Princes...Princesses...
London Castles...New York Mansions...
To live the life of a royal!

In 2002, Harlequin Books lets you escape to a
world of royalty with these royally themed titles:

Temptation:
January 2002—*A Prince of a Guy* (#861)
February 2002—*A Noble Pursuit* (#865)

American Romance:
The Carradignes: American Royalty (Editorially linked series)
March 2002—*The Improperly Pregnant Princess* (#913)
April 2002—*The Unlawfully Wedded Princess* (#917)
May 2002—*The Simply Scandalous Princess* (#921)
November 2002—*The Inconveniently Engaged Prince* (#945)

Intrigue:
The Carradignes: A Royal Mystery (Editorially linked series)
June 2002—*The Duke's Covert Mission* (#666)

Chicago Confidential
September 2002—*Prince Under Cover* (#678)

The Crown Affair
October 2002—*Royal Target* (#682)
November 2002—*Royal Ransom* (#686)
December 2002—*Royal Pursuit* (#690)

Harlequin Romance:
June 2002—*His Majesty's Marriage* (#3703)
July 2002—*The Prince's Proposal* (#3709)

Harlequin Presents:
August 2002—*Society Weddings* (#2268)
September 2002—*The Prince's Pleasure* (#2274)

Duets:
September 2002—*Once Upon a Tiara/Henry Ever After* (#83)
October 2002—*Natalia's Story/Andrea's Story* (#85)

Celebrate a year of royalty with
Harlequin Books!

Available at your favorite retail outlet.

HARLEQUIN®
Makes any time special ®

Visit us at www.eHarlequin.com

COOPER'S CORNER

The newest continuity from Harlequin Books continues in September 2002 with

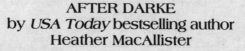

AFTER DARKE
by *USA Today* bestselling author
Heather MacAllister

Check-in: A blind date goes from bad to worse for small-town plumber Bonnie Cooper and city-bred columnist Jaron Darke. When they witness a mob hit outside a restaurant, they are forced to hide out at Twin Oaks. Their cover: they're engaged!

Checkout: While forced to live together in close quarters, these two opposites soon find one thing in common: *passion!*

HARLEQUIN®
Makes any time special ®

Visit us at www.cooperscorner.com

CC-CNM2R

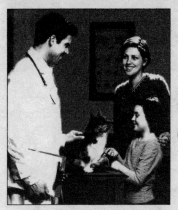